HOLY SMOKE

by Tonino Benacquista

Translated from the French by

Adriana Hunter

BITTER LEMON PRESS
LONDON

BITTER LEMON PRESS

First published in the United Kingdom in 2004 by
Bitter Lemon Press, 37 Arundel Gardens, London W11 2LW

www.bitterlemonpress.com

First published in French as *La Commedia des Ratés* by
Éditions Gallimard. Paris, 1991

This book is supported by the French Ministry for
Foreign Affairs, as part of the Burgess programme
administered by the Institut Français du Royaume-Uni
on behalf of the French Embassy in London and by
the French Ministry of Culture (Centre National
du Livre); publié avec le concours du Ministère
des Affaires Etrangères (Programme Burgess) et
du Ministère de La Culture (Centre National du Livre)

Liberté • Égalité • Fraternité
RÉPUBLIQUE FRANÇAISE

A CIP record for this book is available from the British Library

ISBN 1–904738–01–X

Typeset by RefineCatch Limited, Bungay, Suffolk
Printed and bound by WS Bookwell, Finland

Tonino Benacquista, born in France of Italian immigrants, dropped out of film studies to finance his writing career. After being, in turn, museum nightwatchman, train guard on the Paris–Rome line and professional parasite on the Paris cocktail circuit, he is now a highly successful author of fiction and film scripts. *Holy Smoke* won three prestigious crime fiction awards: the Grand Prix de la Littérature Policière, the Prix Mystère de la Critique and the Trophé 813.

To Cesar and Elena,
Giovanni, Clara, Anna, Iolanda,
and tutti quanti

Italians don't travel.
They emigrate.

Paolo Conte

"Are you coming over to eat on Sunday?"

"Can't . . . I've got work to do."

"Even on a Sunday . . .? *Porca miseria*!"

I don't like it when he gets riled, the old patriarch. But I like going there on a Sunday even less. It's the day when the suburbs pretend to come to life, when everyone's coming out of church and the bookmakers. The two places I try to avoid, even if it means making a detour, so that I don't have to shake hands awkwardly with people who knew me when I was little and who want to know how I'm getting on now. The wops want to know what's become of everyone.

"I'll try to come on Sunday . . ."

My father shakes his head to show that he couldn't care less. He's due to head off on his cure soon; he'll be gone a good month, like every summer, to heal his leg. He'd like me to come by before he leaves. Any father would.

My mother says nothing, as usual. But I know I'll hardly get my foot through the door and she won't be able to stop herself, she'll be telling me loudly, out in the street:

"You must put the heating on if you get cold at home."

"Yes, Mama."

"And don't go out to restaurants too much in Paris. And if you've got any dirty washing you must bring it with you next time."

1

"Yes, Mama."

"And be careful in the Métro in the evenings."

"Yes . . ."

"And, and . . ."

And, and I stop listening, I'm out of earshot. The Pianetas' dog is barking at me. I set off down the little slope which heads towards the bus stop, the bus towards the Métro, and the Métro towards home.

In Paris.

Further up, by the first bungalow in the street, I hear a shrill sound which brings memories flooding back more acutely than a smell washing over you unexpectedly.

"Walking past like a stranger, are you, Antonio . . ."

I wouldn't have been able to recognize him by smell, he now gives off the delicate perfume of some classy aftershave. It feels odd seeing him there, stiffer than the lamppost he's leaning against, the one we used to try and knock down by throwing stones at it on Thursdays, after catechism.

"Dario . . .?" I ask, as if hoping it's someone else.

Despite the years he's still got his angel-in-love good looks. He's even grown better looking. I would guess he's had those teeth replaced, the ones that were missing by the time he was eighteen.

"Your mother said you came over to eat sometimes."

We don't shake hands. I can't remember whether his mother's dead or not. Who could I ask him for news of? Himself, I suppose. So, Dario? Still such a . . . such a . . . wop? What else could I ask him . . .?

Out of the whole gang of kids that we were back then, he – Dario Trengoni – was the only one who'd seen the light of day back there, between Rome and Naples. You couldn't say as much for the Franchini brothers, or the Cuzzo boy or even me. My parents had

2

conceived me as an Italian but in a different South – the South of Paris. And thirty years later they still can't speak the language. Neither can Dario Trengoni, but he wanted it that way. We tried to integrate him, our Dario, into the community at Vitry-sur-Seine: school, benefits, residence permit, social security, the lot. But he refused to be properly integrated into France. He chose to cultivate everything I wanted to get away from, he managed to turn himself into this caricature of a wop, this export-model *vitellone* that you can't even find back there any more. His old mother who'd uprooted herself had acclimatized to our country of asylum much better than him.

"In Paris, is that where you live?"

I don't know what to say. I live in Paris, or in Paris I live. Both are true.

Silence. I'm making so little effort that it's almost embarrassing. He's behaving as if we're sharing something special, a special reunion.

"Do you remember Osvaldo?"

"Yeah . . . is he . . . is he married?"

"He went all American, over there in California, you know . . . He came back here, I saw him, and he's poorer than you or me! He's building himself a house, here . . . He never did have big ideas . . ."

I'm beginning to wish I'd got away sooner. I can't leave just like that, he's been waiting here a long time, for sure. Us meeting on a street-corner like this isn't really a coincidence. In the old days he would sometimes wait a whole morning for one of us to go out and buy the bread, and we knew where we could find him if we were more than usually bored. We used him as a sort of spare friend if the others were busy or being punished. Osvaldo, for example, the one who was ashamed that his name was Osvaldo. And Dario likes that, the fact that one of his old friends from the ghetto can't make his way out. As for me, I find it really irritating that these old friends from the ghetto keep such a close eye on one another.

Dario, it's cold, I'm fed up with standing here, in the wind, going over memories that I forgot as soon as I could, so close to my bus, and that's at least the sixth one that's gone past. Are you any better than Osvaldo yourself? Do you still make people laugh with your shirt unbuttoned to show your crucifix and your red good luck charm? Have you found a way of paying for the Cerruti threads and the Gucci shoes you always dreamed of? Do you still get down on your knees so readily when a girl goes past in the street? Do you still sing the whole time? Do you still believe in your great god Travolta?

Dario Trengoni gave up on his dreams of singing, I gave up on the area where we all grew up, and then we have to meet here, near the lamppost on which we used to scratch out hearts with the initials of the girls next door. French girls. Through the black paint you could see the rust-resistant undercoat. A dirty red. Dirty red hearts.

He serves up another anecdote, but I think he's inventing this one. Dario may not speak French well, but you couldn't say that he masters Italian any better. At the time he used to talk in a strange sort of language that only the local kids understood. The bulk of the sentence was in Roman dialect, with a couple of slang adjectives from the Communist suburbs of Paris, Portuguese apostrophes and Arab commas nicked from the inner city, a sprinkling of back-slang and a few words of our own which we'd invented or poached from the TV or comic strips. At the time I thought it was like a secret code with overtones of mystery and

4

the occult. And I liked the fact that we could cut ourselves off from everyone else right in the middle of the school playground. Now all he has is the pure dialect from home, hybridized with increasingly basic French. The dialect he speaks is called Ciociaro, after a big suburb of Rome. The one they speak in De Sica's films. I've forgotten all of it, I don't speak the language any more. I don't like languages which lean so heavily on sentimentality.

When I think that our fathers travelled 900 miles, from one suburb to another . . .

"Well, it's nice to see you again, Dario . . . must get back . . ."

"*Ashpet'o*! You can *ashpetta* a bit, why I have to speak to you . . ."

In Italian they use the same word for why and because. If Dario ever gets his grammar right, it's always in the wrong language.

"Why you, Anto', you've done *gli studi*, and I haven't done *gli studi*, and you've been to university in Paris. You're *intelligento* . . ."

Not a good sign for me. If Dario Trengoni is keen to tell me I'm intelligent, then he must think I'm thick. What he calls university was in fact two painful years at poly which snuck me onto the job market a bit sooner than expected. But my mother boasted about it all round the neighbourhood.

"Anto', I need you to write me a nice letter, really properly."

"Who to?"

"To Italy."

"Do you still know someone there?"

"*A paio d'amici.*"

"You speak Italian better than I do, I've forgotten it, and anyway, your mates speak in dialect, and you just

5

try writing in dialect, I tell you . . . Ask my father, he could do it, and it'll keep him busy. He's bored, my old man, he'd think it was fun."

"Not possible. I respect *lo* Cesare, he's happy. I don't want to give him something to think about, and anyway . . . I've been waiting nine days for you to go past here. Nine days. You're the only person I can ask. *L'unico.*"

The irresistible ring of truth. It doesn't fill me with joy. I'm delighted to be the only person for someone, but not for some bloke I never see any more. If he's been waiting nine days it could mean that I am this rare creature. It could also mean that there's no big rush.

"What's this letter got to say then?"

"I've got the paper and the envelope, we can buy a stamp at the tabac. I can pay you by the hour if you like."

"What's the letter got to say?"

"In *mezzo alla strada*?"

In the middle of the road? Yes, it's true, we are actually in the middle of the road, the road that goes to the bus stop, but which does go past the tabac, and I will never set foot in that tabac again in my life. I know that Dario still goes there.

"Where are we going?" I ask.

"Not to my place, not *al tabaccho*, too many people. I'll take the bus with you, to Paris."

"No."

"No?"

"I'll be back on Sunday."

"Too late. We're doing this letter right now – your mother says sometimes she makes the tagliatelle and you don't come. So I know what we'll do, we'll go to the *casa 'l diavolo*."

A long time since I've heard that. To the house of the devil. It's the expression our mothers use when they mean: to the devil, to the ends of the earth . . . But the Italians have to put houses everywhere, even in hell. A proper bit of wasteland, like you get round here, a muddy, fallow field behind the boat factory. A good little plot of jungle which acted, and still does, as a cemetery for speedboat hulls. A delight for every aspiring Tarzan and Captain Flint. Two cherry trees. A lilac. A smell of resin lingering over the rubbish and wreckage.

"I'll get dirty," I say, slipping under the fence.

Dario doesn't hear, he's making sure no one sees us go in, but not like earlier, he's no longer got a face like a spy that you could spot a mile off.

I can't make out whether anything's changed. I'm sure wastelands can't be what they used to be. Dario climbs into a twenty-six-foot hull and I follow him.

"You can lean on here."

He takes out a pad of paper and a blue ballpoint pen.

Dario isn't thinking how much resin went into making this twenty-six-foot shell. He's forgotten that his father died after fifteen years of inhaling the fumes from this shit, which trashes your lungs. My father refused straight away, he was happier wrapping the boats in straw casings. Maybe it reminded him of harvesting. The unions have now made gas masks compulsory. At the time they used to make the workers drink a carton of milk a day. Old man Trengoni must have drunk whole swimming pools of the stuff to ward off the toxic fumes.

I'd forgotten about that.

Dario settles himself into a recess where we used to imagine the helm and the radio. And I go to the side that's least overrun by moss. To starboard.

7

"Is it long, what you've got to say?"

"Quite, yes . . . Are you comfortable? At the top on the left-hand side put . . . no . . . higher than that . . . you're leaving too much space, a bit less . . . there . . . do it nicely . . . Dear Madame Raphaëlle, at the top, with a nice big R."

"In French?"

"Yes."

"But you said it was for a friend back there."

"Nah, it's for a woman, a woman who's a friend," he said, looking like an embarrassed child, a real child.

For the time being I give up trying to understand. Why bother, anyway? How could I refuse to write a love letter for an illiterate? My father definitely wouldn't have been able to help him. If it really is a love letter, then nine days must be too long. And it even seems possible that I might be the one and only person Dario knows who has some idea of where to put those subtle dot, dot, dots in a love letter to a French woman.

"Now, we've got to tell her that I don't always tell *la bucia . . . la bucia . . .*?"

"Lies."

"That's it . . . Tell her that sometimes I tell the truth, especially at the end. In the beginning, we didn't meet by chance. I knew that she sometimes went to the club on her own. Go on, write . . . ."

"You don't realize what you're asking me to do, Dario. To write something without understanding, without knowing what's going on, none of it."

"Go on, write . . . but write nicely, with a bit of . . . *un poco di cuore, andiamo*, go on . . ."

I start scratching. The blue ink only just moistens the tip of the pen.

"'Dear Madame Raphaëlle, I have not always been a liar. When we first met it was not by chance.' Is that all right?"

He scrutinizes every last upstroke as if afraid he's being betrayed. *Traduttore traditore.*

"*Bene, bene, andiamo,* don't bother about the club. Tell her thank you for the ticket and the money for America, and for everything else."

"Have you been to the States, then?"

He lowers his eyes towards the wheel on a trailer.

"Once, that's all."

"Did you work there?"

"Write it down!"

I recreate his sentence almost word for word, including the vague bits, but my version seems to satisfy him.

"After that say that I'm going to pay back as much as I can, if I have the time, that is."

"Do you mean if you 'find' the time or if you're 'given' the time?"

"Isn't it the same?"

"Not really."

"Well, say I'll do it as quickly as possible, but maybe the others'll be quicker than me, put that . . . She'll understand *a menta sua,* in her own mind . . ."

A few crossings out.

"Don't worry, I'll copy it out afterwards . . ."

He can tell that I'm struggling. I'm really beginning to see why I was the only one.

"Tell her that it's not over. You have to believe in *miracoli* and that *lo miracolo . . . si svolgéra . . .*"

The miracle will come to pass . . .

A song lyric. Ridiculous. He's poached that from a Gianni Morandi song, or something like that. I can even remember the tune.

"It's nearly finished, Anto'. Now you've got to do the most important bit. Make it so she understands that *la mia strada è lunga, proprio lunga* . . . and that she and I will meet up *a qualche parte della strada*."

Now there I had to think for a bit. And I put the lid back on the pen. My road is long and we will find each other somewhere along it . . . I refuse to write stuff like that. There are limits. He's come up with this meta- phor and he's going to squeeze it out of the poor ball- point pen, but it's like some terrible dirge from Celentano.

"What do you mean exactly? Your 'road' is long . . . Do you mean, I don't know . . . the path of life or something like that . . .?"

He stares at me warily.

"*Ma sei pazzo* . . .? You're mad, Antonio! I'm talking about the road, our road, the road you were born in, the one back there, where your parents and my mother live, the Rue Anselme-Rondenay in Vitry-sur- Seine. That's the one you've got to put in the letter!"

"Don't get annoyed or I'll stop. And why do you want to say that it's long, it's clear you've never got away from the place. Are you sure you've been to the States?"

"Write what I said, our road, it's practically the long- est road in the world . . . You're the only one in the neighbourhood who hasn't grasped that, Anto', that's why you left for Parigi. Go on, write it down . . ."

Mute, muddled, bewildered, I go ahead. The pen can't make up its mind to write the simplest sentence ever to alight on a white page. What's this Madame Raphaëlle going to read into all this? Four little words I don't know how to go about saying.

And I try to convince myself that the message that all the poets in the world have tried to convey in thousands of pages, over the centuries, that ultimate, despairing wisdom ... Well, it would take a moronic, uneducated little wop to try and capture it in four pathetic words.

My road is long.

*   *   *

I handed him the letter, and he copied it out, concentrating like a little kid, really neatly, just the way he wanted, having taken it from my hand without a thank you. Then he sealed it in an envelope and wrote an address on it, turning as far away from me as possible. Right over to port.

"Go on, Anto', go and get your bus. And don't tell anyone about this – swear on your mother's head."

I jumped, feet together, into the imaginary sea with its flotsam of breeze blocks smothered in couch grass. Dario waited till I was some way away before abandoning ship.

"Have you done something stupid, Dario?"

From down below I could only see his hand, hanging on to the rail.

"Tell me, have you done something stupid?"

I walked out of the jungle without waiting for the answer he would never give me, and I made my way back onto the Rue Anselme-Rondenay.

From the top of the rise I looked back down on it, I got it in perspective. Seven hundred, maybe eight hundred feet, top whack. About thirty neat little bungalows made the Italian way, with endless patience and bricks laid late into the night. I was born down that road. Whether I like it or not, I can't help being a part of it.

I won't come back on Sunday.

Dario Trengoni had better not ask me for anything else.

I'm going home.

To Paris. And the road is long.

Leaning on my balcony, I scoured the landscape trying to make out the arrowhead of Notre-Dame through the aerials. When I moved in, the previous tenant assured me that he had seen it in clear weather on the stroke of 10 a.m. I live opposite the Salons Laroche, a place people hire when they want to throw serious parties, which does no favours for the eardrums of the neighbours. I'm the only resident who doesn't complain. I was about to climb up on a stool when a cleaning woman on the terrace opposite, dragging a bin full of rubbish from the night before, tried to dissuade me.

"That would be stupid, at your age. Just think, it's nearly summer."

A rustling on the doormat outside told me that I had some mail, and I waited a while for the concierge to move away. The telephone rang just as I was opening the door. But I had time to see the thing, so white, so black and so inert it seemed to claw my eyes as I put my hand out towards it.

The ringing went on.

On the other end, one of my sisters. I called her Clara but it was actually Yolande. My father would have said Anna. One chance in three, but you always lose.

"Antoine . . . Do you know what?"

"Someone's dead."

"You know already?"

I asked her to hang on for a minute. My heart raced and I went back to pick up the thing with its black

13

edging. Someone was dead inside there. I just had to open the envelope to find out their name. I wondered whether it would be better to read it or to be told it. I hesitated, for a moment, with the telephone in one hand and the announcement in the other. To read it or to be told it? Both would make me feel sick, without really knowing why.

Actually, no, I do know why. It's because the dead man and I had already died a thousand times together on the battlefield, giving each other the coup de grâce every time the cavalry didn't get there on time, challenging each other to duels, ten paces apart, facing each other, taking turns. We would freeze bolt upright for three seconds, our faces disfigured by a grimace, before collapsing to the ground.

And to think it was nearly summer.

"It's Trengoni," I said towards the mouthpiece.

"I saw his mother yesterday, on my way to Mum and Dad. Are you going to go, to the funeral? She'd really like it if you were there, Trengoni's mother."

"Why?"

" . . . What do you mean why? That makes you a bit of a bastard even to ask . . . you were mates, weren't you?"

Then she told me how Dario had died.

But I didn't want to believe it. That's not how childhood friends die.

* * *

Mothers, gaggles of them. His, not far from the hole and the priest; mine, a long way away in the hierarchy of suffering, and all the others, with or without their offspring, boys mostly. I feel as if I'm reading the announcement again: Mr and Mrs *cosi, cosa, coso, cosello, cosieri, cosatello*, and their children . . .

14

Practically everyone's there, except for my father, because of his gammy leg. Old Mother Trengoni won't have seen the last of this cemetery, she'll be visiting with her husband and her now only son. She must be wondering whether leaving for France was a good move. Knowing her, she'll never have another chance to go back to her village – she won't want to leave her two men.

My sisters haven't come, nor my brother; no one really knew Dario. Just a colourful figure in the neighbourhood. They all thought I was the only one amongst us with a legitimate place in the funeral procession. Dario and I used to come out of school and hide, so we could laugh like drains at the coffins going past to the cemetery, the Cimetière du Progrès (the Cemetery of Progress, ha!). It was in the Rue du Progrès, you see, behind the estate of high-rise council blocks. With the same name.

I've got a grandfather in the next row. To escape from the weight of silence I look around for the cast-iron cross my father brought back from the factory for him. Dario's is very simple, just his name and his dates. I try to see how many faces I don't know in the gathering, and I make out four or five. There are a few clouds coming in from the North. All we need now is rain, in the middle of summer. The priest is about to stop preaching. The bit everyone dreads is coming, when you file past the mother, when those who are really suffering will hold her to them, and those who are really inspired will come out with a little sentence all about down here below, and up there above and, of course, over there, a load of well-meaning bullshit which won't comfort anyone, but it's not very often that people round here go in for metaphysics. Some people pick up the aspergillum and sprinkle a little holy water, but I'm more interested in the others, the ones who hang back, those who don't dare but who have got as far as this Cimetière du Progrès, hidden away in a left-wing suburb. Shall I go to the aspergillum or not? There's this woman with her face hidden by a veil, just there on my left. She's sniffing loudly, probably a little too much, I can't stand the way southerners are so demonstrative. If you're going to put your heart into crying like that, you must have some right to. She already reeks of a *mater dolorosa*. But I can hardly see anything of her, not her eyes, or her legs, and some intuition tells me that this woman isn't crying Italian tears, but real French ones. Standing there with her hands in front of her mouth, you can't actually tell if she's crying or praying.

Dario? Dario? Who is she then? Don't tell me you actually managed to catch yourself a French girl to top off your career as the local Latin lover? Did you hear what the priest had to say about you? Did it sound about right, what he said about how cheerful you were and about the memories you would leave us with? Would you like me to give you a funeral oration? You were nothing more than a good-looking lad just waiting for the world to realize it, you were too lazy to become a petty criminal and too proud to knead pizza dough. What was good about you? Not much, apart from your luminous ideas about trying to *cavarsela* as you called it, finding a little space in the sun, finding a niche. But without having to dig. Well, other people took care of digging out your niche today, at least you succeeded there. The priest with all his kind words doesn't suspect that he was your first victim, before you were even ten. The fake tombola tickets at the church bazaar. And you spent all the money betting on the horses. And does anyone remember your turn on the radio talent show at the spring fête? You came second after a rock-group on the stage. You sang, hand on heart, some old number by Boby Solo: *Una lacrima sul viso* . . . My father ended up in tears too, he was laughing so much. And you, queen for a day, you thought it was okay. There, those are the memories you leave us with, a succession of unlikely schemes whose only merit was that they never actually cost you a spell in jail.

There was no need to end up lying in there so soon. I haven't told anyone about your letter, but I haven't managed to forget. They say you died of a gunshot to the head, that you were found on the quays by the Seine, right on the edge of Ivry. Do you think I was surprised? I can't bring myself to believe you didn't do something really stupid, after all that stuff you made me write. I can't help thinking that you may have deserved it, the gunshot I mean, like you deserved the thrashings you had as a kid. And what was this money you had to pay back "if you found the time"? Was this the desperate promise that was finally going to make a man of you?

And her, here, on my left? She's crying like a girl called Raphaëlle. She's managed to find all the tears I didn't know how to look for. We're not measuring grief on the same scale. And there's not much of mine.

But I'm not the only one. There's a couple of blokes leaning up against the plane trees about thirty feet away, one in shirt sleeves, the other in a jacket. Something tells me that pair aren't exactly wracked with grief. How many of us are there like that? I only just managed to avoid the aspergillum, but I did kiss Mrs Trengoni. It's not as if I really wanted to but I'm the same age as the son she's lost, and with my dark eyes and dark hair, I thought she might want to dry her cheeks against mine for a moment.

She held me to her so tightly that I felt imprisoned by her pain.

* * *

The afternoon was terribly long. My mother gave me strict instructions to stay in the area for as long as was needed, without actually giving me a valid reason. My father was less vehement but he still asked me to make an effort. I could tell that it was serious when he abandoned his dialect for a clearer, purer form of Italian, a Tuscan strain that he only uses to talk about important things. As if he was abandoning his peasant talk to become a gentleman, a *signore*, in short, someone with some credibility. At times like these, his use of the polite third person gives me the creeps. My mother gave us an espresso that threatened us with tachycardia, and he explained what was expected of me.

Old Mother Trengoni will not be left to grieve in peace. The police aren't really sure how to proceed with a devastated old woman who only speaks in some jargon which is pretty much incomprehensible even to the "foreigners" who live just a stone's throw from her native village. They still haven't succeeded in interviewing her since the body was found; each time they unleash a tragedy of Greek proportions and end up drenched in tears. I try to imagine two policemen grappling with a fat woman wailing in some unknown language and refusing to accept the idea of a bullet in her son's head. They need an interpreter, one who also happens to have known the deceased well. The perfect interviewee, in other words . . . She could only come up with one name.

18

Dario had asked me to translate Italian into French, and now the police were going to ask me to go the other way, and I just can't seem to get away from this language I've been trying to forget for such a long time. No one can imagine how much I hate juggling with the looping nuances of a language that no longer inspires any real respect in me. From Italian into French just about works, but going from French into Italian . . . I can turn *E così sia* into "And so it was", but it would take me hours to reverse the process. And this horror of translating into Italian is based on the fact that I've already been through this purgatory, in its most extreme form, at the Gustave Roussy Cancer Treatment Centre. On my way to see a friend, I stopped for a moment in front of a poster asking for volunteers bilingual in French and Italian to help with the forty per cent of their patients who have come from every corner of the peninsula. Wops trust mechanics more than they do doctors. I naively felt that, as and when I came, I could be useful to distressed patients who didn't understand a single word of the doctors' terrible revelations. A little bit of help; it would be simple, kind, inconsequential.

Big mistake, huge.

News of my application spread through the entire floor like wildfire. Women would come up to me on their own, completely bald, or with bald children, in wheelchairs, and men holding their drips in one hand. The new arrivals, the cancer immigrants, full of their hows and whys and how longs. An avalanche of words, a tornado of hopes, a magma of fear – and all that held back by the slender thread of language. Each of them bearing down on me, telling me their story, forcing me into their urgent intimate details. I coped pretty well; the nurses managed to answer the first questions, the simpler ones, about rooms and meals, the running of the hospital and the forms that needed filling out. A doctor asked me to follow him into a particular room just for a few minutes, to see a woman he had operated on the day before for a facial tumour. The knot in my stomach which was still relatively slack suddenly tightened. How do you say "tumour" again? When I saw the woman with her head wrapped in gauze I could tell that the worst was still to come. Translating into Italian. The doctor asked me to explain to her what the rest of her life would be like. Getting the wrong adjective or choosing a duff adverb were just not options . . . Trying to be as accurate as possible in another language, reconstituting the icy precision of the surgeon's prognosis.

"Tell her the operation went well, and that all the cancerous cells have gone."

I translate as best I can, she understands, she nods, I can breathe.

"Tell her that we'll take the bandages off in about ten days. But tell her also that the tumour was bigger than we expected and that, even with very good plastic surgery, we'll never be able to get rid of the cavity in her left cheek."

That's when I severed all links with that language.

A white shirt and a jacket. I wasn't surprised when I saw them again in there, sitting at a table with a yellow waxed cloth covered in burns from the cafetière. One of them's studying an old calendar on the table, pushing aside the palm frond which is shedding its leaves on the month of March. The old woman is there, a bit to one side, with her black veil pushed back over her forehead. She wanted me to sit next to her, while she kneaded my right hand, and the inspectors behaved as if they thought that was quite normal. I introduced myself as a former friend of Dario's; we agreed on how difficult it was to communicate with the old girl and they thanked me straight away for my help before even asking the first question. The police who worked in the Vitry-sur-Seine community, with its thirty-five thousand immigrants from all over the place, have to deal with this sort of thing every day. They were discreet and understanding, only making me translate clear and simple questions which could have been reduced to just one: who was Dario? The description that the priest had given of him that morning can't have been of much help to them. What he did, what he lived on, who he saw, his salary. The old girl had never known anything about all that, that was the problem. But he did live here with you . . .? He went out in the mornings, he sometimes came back in the evenings, he never did anything wrong. I explained to the police that, to an Italian *mamma*, seeing her son come home before nightfall was like definitive proof of his honesty.

"Did he have any enemies?"

"*Aveva nemici?*"

"No! No!"

My nerves were on edge so I took out a cigarette and picked up a blue plastic lighter lying on the table.

After a good hour of this little game of questions without answers, the policeman in the jacket got bored and sneakily shifted the interrogation towards me. I told him everything I knew about Dario, which wasn't much in fact, and I thought it just as well to leave out our last meeting and the business with the letter. Why did I do that? For two very simple reasons: I'd given Dario my word that I would keep my trap shut for the rest of my days. But also, I was particularly frightened that by just mentioning this money which needed paying back so urgently and this Madame Raphaëlle, I would definitely make myself the number one lead in their enquiry. And I really don't want to be a lead.

"Does she remember the evening of the 22nd of July? He ate here. What time did he go out?"

She thought for a long time, with tears in her eyes. She had made supper, he didn't eat a thing, he went out at about eight o'clock and never came home again, that was it.

"Are you sure he didn't touch his supper? What had you made?"

I thought the question was completely insignificant compared to the others.

"*Pasta asciutta.*"

"That's pasta without any sauce, or hardly any," I said.

The two inspectors looked at each other, sceptically. One of them explained to me that, with murders, there is always an autopsy. From what was found in Dario's stomach they knew that, two hours before he was killed, he had eaten some pasta. And, apparently, nothing else. I almost asked them what sort of pasta it was, but for a moment I imagined the cloying magma they had found inside him.

"It would seem that he ate it somewhere else; there was also some maize and a herb which might have been mint."

"And dandelion, too," added the other one.

"Yup, dandelion. That's not this pasta-chutta is it? Ask her if her son could have found that lot in the fridge, some leftovers, I don't know . . ."

When I mentioned the maize, the dandelions and the mint, the old woman looked at me as if I was talking about cyanide. No, Mamma Trengoni had never made that in her life. No Italian woman in the world

22

would mix up something that disgusting. How could Dario have eaten it? I'm pretty sure that not one of those ingredients features in any pasta recipe. There's something I'm not getting.

"Ask her if her son had a gun."

I already knew the answer.

"And you, Mr Polsinelli, he never showed you a fire-arm, a revolver? The bullet that killed him was a nine millimetre."

"I never saw him with anything like that in his hand," I said. "And I don't know anything about that sort of thing."

Mamma Trengoni had suddenly had enough. "Tell them to fuck off," she told me in her patois. I've never had any luck with that language.

As if they had understood, they moved away, mutter-ing to me that the old woman hadn't been much help. They thanked me again, made a note of my telephone number and left at about 11 p.m. I was about to follow them when Mamma Trengoni held me back with the clammy red hand she had been kneading me with throughout the proceedings. She wanted to talk to me privately about him, in her strange jargon which was beginning to sound increasingly normal to me.

"Will you give me your telephone number, too, Antonio . . .?"

How could I refuse? I wouldn't have had time. She handed me a piece of paper and opened a drawer in the table where I saw a heap of ballpoint pens, all iden-tical and in the same blue as the cigarette lighter I'd been using all afternoon. I took a second look and realized that the pen Dario had given me to write the letter came from the same drawer. She gave me one and I scribbled my number down. Paper and pen bore the same name, advertised in gothic letters: The Up.

Private Club. 43, Rue George-V. The sort of address that was more likely to relate to the son than the mother. I put the pen into the breast pocket of my black suit jacket.

"Dario should have stayed with you. You were a good friend. He should have gone to Paris and found a job, instead of hanging around here. Three months ago he told me he wanted to go back to the homeland, to Sora, to cultivate our little vineyard. That would have been better for him. Paris or Sora. But not here. *In questra strada di merda . . .*"

I dropped in on my parents to report back as expected. My mother had cooked some turnip tops, and some odd-shaped pasta in chicken stock. Didn't have the heart to make a proper sauce, she said. I sipped a little bit of stock straight from the pan on the paraffin stove, and my father turned the sound down on the TV so as not to miss any of what I was saying. I had to grin and bear it: I felt like all of Paris was waiting for me, like my black suit and tie might end up in the fire, like I'd soon see the end of this day of suburban mourning, so sad it's enough to kill me too.

I gave a basic account of the interview and asked the old man what a nine-millimetre calibre was, in case he actually remembered, but he didn't deign to reply.

"The funny thing is that Dario said he wanted to tend the vineyard. Apparently the Trengonis have got a plot of land over there?"

"The vineyard over by Sant'Angelo?" he asked nervously.

"I dunno."

"*Cretino . . .*"

I talked about the pasta that had been found in the dead man's stomach, and on the strength of that the old man got up on his one good leg and hobbled over to me. He tried to hide his surprise and asked me to repeat it.

"Repeat what?"

"Maize."

"Ugh . . . yes. Before he died he ate a pasta dish with maize in it."

"And what else?"

"They mentioned mint . . . and dandelions."

He stood silent for a moment, deep in thought, then he asked for a chair and sat down facing me. He told me to stop sipping the soup for a moment.

"Maize, dandelions and mint . . .? Are you sure . . .?"

"Of course . . . I'd never heard of it. What d'you think, Mamma? You've never made that, have you?"

My mother, feeling a little uneasy, swore before God that she had never put those three ingredients together in a pan. She doesn't even know what mint is. She asked straight away what kind of pasta they had found.

"*Pasta fina o pasta grossa?*"

I told her what any forensic scientist would have said: who knows . . .

The old man suddenly started muttering shapeless syllables as if he were drunk, then limped back off towards the little sideboard to take out the bottle of grappa. Before my mother had time to intervene he had taken several gulps straight from the bottle and had frozen for a moment to let the burning pass. He isn't allowed to drink from that bottle and he knows it, but my mother must have sensed that, on this particular evening, he wouldn't tolerate any remonstrances. And it's none of my business now, except that I was intrigued by this sudden urge to knock back something strong.

As he put the bottle away he said just one word.

"Rigatoni . . ."

A momentary stunned silence . . .

"What do you . . . What are you talking about rigatoni for?"

"Because that's what he ate. Rigatoni."

"How do you know that?"

"Because I say so."

The sort of definitive argument he liked using.

"For God's sake, explain, *porco Giuda*!"

Rigatoni is quite a large pasta shape, with a hole
through it and ridges so that it gets really impregnated
with sauce. A big enough calibre to split a family
in two, those for and those against, and in our house
our father took sole charge of the against. He's always
loathed pasta that you eat one piece at a time and
which fills up your whole mouth. He's a fervent
defender of capellinis, the finest form of spaghetti,
cut in three and cooked in a matter of seconds.
Whether it's the agile slaloming motion of the fork
through the squiggling entropy, or the strange fluid
sensation in the throat, either way he won't budge. He
conceals his dislike when Mamma makes rigatoni. But
from that to implying it killed Dario is pushing it.

"What on earth are you talking about?" I ask in a
high-pitched voice, with a half smile.

His only reply is to switch the TV back on and to
settle himself in his armchair. The barrel organ music
of the film-club on Channel Two creates an odd
atmosphere.

"Leave me alone, I'm watching the film."

With a discreet wave of her hand, my mother asks
me to drop it. She knows him better than me, after all.

I mustn't miss the last bus. Before leaving I kiss my
father, who shouldn't have to wait much longer to get
his leg fixed.

"When are you off on your cure?"

"*Domani mattina*," says my mother. "And I can't wait
. . ." she adds without him hearing.

I'm on the doorstep but for some reason I'm hesitat-
ing, me who never needs any encouragement to leave
this place. I've got to tackle it again. One last time.

"Come on, what's the story with the rigatoni . . .?"

He leapt to his feet and shouted – I expected anything but that – and he bellowed at me, calling me a
cretin and ordering me to leave, to go home, to Paris,
screaming that I didn't have any business there in that
house.

My mother left the room, perhaps to get away from
his anger, and he was off again, saying it was bad
enough having to go away for his cure, and there was
no one there to help her. Eventually he said that
sooner or later I could end up the same way as Dario.

The whole bit. An exceptional performance.

While all this rancour was spewing out, I kept my
eyes on the TV. Anything to avoid looking meekly
down at the floor. When he chucked me out, I still
didn't know why he'd targeted me. On the other
hand, I did realize why he was so keen to see that evening's film, *The March on Rome*. The story of two fascist
apprentices indoctrinating each other over a plate of
polenta.

It was like some war memory.

* * *

Tossing and turning in my sheets, by the end of the
night I had a bit of a fever. With memories of Dario
scalding my forehead as I waited for dawn. He had to
wait till he was underground before coming and
haunting me in my sleep. Half asleep I imagine the

27

moment of his death, in slow motion, as a duel between two actors, one of them ill-lit and indistinct, the other grimacing as best he can while – thanks to special effects – he realizes that his brains have just splattered against the wall. A very bad ending. It wound me up. I opened my eyes with a start and got up to go and see what was going on under my window. Not much, the usual party-goers on the terrace opposite, the dustbin lorry, a car starting up, a faint light just hazing the darkness. Four-thirty, too early for anything, especially for getting to work, even if I am lucky enough to work from home. I look at the polystyrene model I've been commissioned by some architect to finish before the end of September. There's plenty of time. Too much. It's too early for everything.

But not for a good strong cup of coffee. I wanted to make a really good one, the sort I'd make for a girl to impress her. Probably my own little way of celebrating the burial of a little wop. Some would have got drunk, I make a cup of coffee that he would have drunk as a connoisseur. Mineral water with just a pinch of salt. The coffee is a Colombian blend which I grind quite coarsely, because of the hot weather. I put the filter into the reservoir and screw on the lid. What do you think of that, Dario? You're pretty surprised I'm so meticulous with coffee. Do you think a mug of dish-water would do for me? You're not going to believe this but espresso's the last link I have with the old country. Tricky phase: dropping one little tear of water in the reservoir so that the first few drops of coffee that come through – the darkest – don't evaporate on the burning hot metal. As soon as they appear I pour them onto a lump of sugar in my cup, and stir it briskly to make a lovely brown emulsion. When the rest of the coffee has come through I fill a whole cup and put the emulsion into it. It stays there in suspension, giving it that special taste you won't find anywhere this side of the Alps. Here's to you, Dario.

Still half asleep, I sipped the nectar for a good fifteen minutes, thinking over that improbable death, and the fact that, apart from the killer himself and the police looking into it, I was the only person who knew any of the details. I delved through what I could remember of the strange letter he sent just before his death. I had weighed up a fair number of theories as carefully as possible when, suddenly, out of nowhere, one word – just one – came to me and started hammering violently in every recess of my memory. A crappy, meaningless word which had become so important in the space of a few seconds. And all of a sudden everything else dropped away from my focus of interest. The word loomed up again and wasn't going to let me go, and that was when I realized that I was properly waking up now, with this word.

Rigatoni.

Rigatoni, rigatoni, rigatoni . . . What did my daft old man mean with his rigatoni? When I told him about the autopsy he went strange for a few seconds but he pulled himself together quickly, then he clammed up like an oyster – he's good at that – and here I am this morning with this word in my head and nothing else means anything at all. The drama was there, in the rigatoni, and that's all there was to it. The old patriarch likes a joke but he wouldn't have made one about the death of a lad he'd practically seen being born. He hadn't been drunk but had tried pretty hard to get drunk straight afterwards. He almost insulted me, for no obvious reason, and then took refuge in his TV and told me to scarper, and that's a bad sign.

I wait so as not to wake them, and it's my mother who answers.

"He's already left, Antonio. After his row with you, his leg was hurting him more than ever."

"How long's he going to be away?"

"Pfff . . . a month, as usual."

"I'll come and see you soon, *ciao* . . ."

The old man had chosen flight. That's what I concluded. Flight from something connected with Dario's death. He would rather set off for Perros-Guirec to have his left groin pummelled, than reply to just one of my questions or confront whatever the hell it was that had stopped both of us sleeping. For me it's not all that serious but he's seventy-two and he's got a leg that doesn't work. Not to mention his tendency to snigger every time a doctor suggests he cuts down on alcohol and tobacco. My father is a cheerful ruin who can't see any reason why that should change. Unless he's put himself out of harm's way . . . how would I know?

The sun's coming up and I'm asking myself the same question as the policemen in the suburbs: who was Dario? The modern Dario, the one of three months ago. The one I could have been if my natural curiosity hadn't nudged me out of the Rue Anselme-Rondenay.

Towards the end of the evening I went over to my sister to borrow her car. At about midnight I hovered around the Rue George-V, not really knowing whether or not I was going to stop. The Up, private club. A blue sign, a black door, a doorbell. Dario mentioned it in his letter. Two words I'm prejudiced against: club and private. Not to mention the name. It sounds like some hostess bar. The décor's bound to be terrible. The bouncer a blockhead. The girls pathetic. And the customers naff. I've already assessed the premises. Made to measure for Dario.

Just in case, I kept my black suit and tie on. It was that sort of place. I rang the bell. The bouncer eyed me for a few seconds. Those guys know what sort of person they're dealing with before they've even set foot over the threshold. He just opened the door, without a smile, without saying a word, and I didn't need to serve up the little sentence I'd concocted for him. A cloakroom where I didn't leave anything. The first bar with a couple of men in the same suit as me, probably the managers or regulars. Like I said, the décor's terrible. The music's coming from downstairs. A faint purring of variety show stuff. With my hands in my pockets I hurry down to the cellar with its red wallpaper, its bench seats and armchairs, a second bar, some Japanese men, and some averagely pretty, averagely sexy girls. I thought that to get people thirsty you had to warm them up first. In a little recess there are five or six men sitting talking without any drinks or girls. Second distinct impression: no one's going to come over to me, I could stand here like this for a long time before anyone came and offered me anything. I sit down on a stool at the bar and it's quite a while before the barman comes over to me.

"Bourbon. Without any ice."

"Jack Daniel's, Wild Turkey, Four Roses, Southern Comfort."

They're all 115 francs a glass, I might as well have the best. I downed it in one, and even slightly regretted not having any ice. Then another. It was at the end of the third that I did the calculation: 345 francs worse off, half an hour of silence, and I still didn't know whether it was a good idea to have come. In the meantime people had been arriving, couples, tourists, more girls, no way of knowing whether or not they worked there. No one wants to talk to me. I'm transparent. Invisible. I don't exist to any of them. The alcohol goes to my head a bit, the room gets busier. I gesture to the barman to get him to come and listen.

"Did you know someone called Dario Trengoni . . .?"

A slight step back, he looks round the room, puts down the glass he was wiping.

"I haven't been here very long. Was he a customer?"

"I don't know."

"Wait a minute."

When I think about it I wonder whether that was a good idea. He comes out from behind the bar and hurries over to the five men sitting in the corner. Five synchronized pairs of eyes turn towards me. The barman comes back.

"Someone's going to find out, don't go away. A little Bourbon while you're waiting?"

"Yes."

Triple shot. I loosen the knot of my tie a little.

"Look over to your left, there's going to be a show in a couple of minutes. You might like it."

A red curtain. Behind it there must be a little stage edged with lights and embedded with pieces of mirror. Just time to empty my glass and the curtain opens. From the glint in the barman's eye, I'd immediately assumed it would be a strip-tease, naff like everything else. But I was wrong again: a young guy appeared in the yellow halo of a spotlight, to feeble scattered applause. Dinner jacket. Mike. Dark good looks. Darkness in the room.

He put his heart into it, this lad. Starting with a song that used to bring tears to my little sister's eyes ten years ago, it went something like *Ti Amo Ti Amo Ti Amo* . . . and pretty much just that for three minutes. Then he segued into *Sei Bellissima* . . . and at that precise moment I realized that this was a true wop, it was the way he dragged out the *Bellissssssima* . . . People gave me nasty looks when I involuntarily burst out laughing. Until I pulled myself together and asked the barman to refill my glass. Which I downed in one. When he intoned *Volare ooooho Cantare*, I finally grasped what Dario had been here. Barman, impossible. Customer, unlikely. Singer. He had succeeded in that, playing the crooner with his old-fashioned charms, and singing sentimental oldies grown threadbare in a hookers' bar. I roared with laughter again as I tried to imagine him. I even thanked him out loud for following his swooning dream, and for sticking to his role as the operetta wop who made the whole neighbourhood laugh.

Dario, I regret all the things I could have said, you saw your dream through and I'm the only one who knows. You should have told me all this last time I saw you alive. You were frightened of looking stupid. And you were wrong . . .

Someone put their hand on my shoulder and it brought me back down with a bump. A man a bit older than the others leant towards my ear and asked me to follow him. It was when I tried to get off my stool that I realized the state I was in. Two guys held me by the elbows and I let them take me behind the curtain. I genuinely thought it was to help me. They sat me down on some cases of bottles. From the wings, I could hear the singer's voice echoing even louder.

"Whata do you want with Dario . . .?"

I opened my eyes wide to try and see his face. The other two let me go.

". . . Nothing . . . He's . . . He's dead . . ."

The excess of alcohol started churning in my stomach.

"I'm looking for a . . . a Madame Rapha . . . Raphaëlle . . ."

33

My eyes kept closing of their own accord, but I struggled not to miss anything.

"Why?"

"What the hell is it to you . . . ?"

I was clouted so quickly that I couldn't tell which of the three of them had hit me. The oldest searched through my jacket, took out my wallet and made off with it. I puked some threads of bile on the red fabric. They dragged me over to a tap and rammed my head under the stream of cold water for a ridiculously long time. It eventually cooled the seething lava in my head. There was only one of them left with me now.

"You're not a policeman, and you're not from the States. What do you want?"

"I was a friend of Dario's."

"That guy . . . a friend . . . ? My arse . . . I'm the one that found him at the dance hall near Montparnasse, he was a taxi-boy there and we needed another singer here, the boss loves that sort of thing, 'specially the mawkish Italian stuff. We didn't have to ask him twice, our Dario."

He spoke so quickly that I missed half of it.

"Taxi-boy?"

"Are you sure you were friends? He danced with people for money if you like. Mind you, maybe he should have stayed there. He earned more there in one weekend . . ."

"Dancing . . .?"

He sniggered.

"Where are you from . . .? Yep, he had some pretty impressive customers, gotta hand it to him . . . they were clamouring at the doors to twirl round the room with Dario, and not just the old biddies. And they clamoured all the more at closing time."

"Don't understand . . ."

34

He sniggered.

"I see," he said knowingly. "Singing and dancing was just public relations, the advertising, the façade. Our Dario could have auctioned himself off to the ladies. Do you know what a guy like that can earn?"

"Dario . . . a gigolo?"

"He wouldn't have liked to be called that. When we heard he was dead, it came as quite a blow, I can tell you. We don't like that sort of thing. He had friends. But that boy didn't want them, all he wanted was money, money, money. Just like everyone else, okay, but with him it didn't even leave time for a quick chat."

"Why did he need so much money?"

"Dunno. A lot and quickly. With his face and his voice he was right to go all out for it, you know. I wouldn't mind looking like him."

"And who's Madame Raphaëlle?"

Too late. The old boy came back and his henchman clammed up straight away. In the background I heard the crooner making a start on *Come Prima*.

"Do your audiences like that sort of song? Even my grandfather thinks that's a bit past it."

He slowly and pointedly put my wallet back, swept his hands over my jacket to knock the creases out of it, and tightened the knot of my tie.

"I like it very much, and that's all that matters. *Capisch?*"

He took me under his arm to lead me back to the front door. People stepped aside as we passed, and I felt like someone important.

"Can you sing, Antonio Polsinelli?"

"No. Not like Dario, anyway."

"Nobody could sing like him. But, if you need work, you could come and see me. You gotta good face from the homeland. *Ciao, ragazzo . . .*"

I found myself back outside, not that I necessarily wanted to be there. With the beginnings of a headache. Before going to find my car I stood motionless for quite a while, leaning against the door to the club, trying to keep my eyes open so that I didn't topple over completely. I could even have lain down in the gutter for a nice little hour, and waited for it to pass.

That's when I saw the car parked right under my nose. A grey metallic Jaguar, huge and silent with one silhouette in the driver's seat and another in the back. I didn't have time to react; the driver climbed out and opened the rear door on the pavement side, without a word. The passenger leaned out. In the half light I couldn't make out the face.

"Monsieur Antonio, I need to talk to you."

From the way she said it, I didn't for a moment think this was a trap. Even if the owner of The Up had had a lot to do with this little meeting. No, in fact, I felt drawn towards this car and its mysterious occupant. Yesterday she had been wearing a black veil and that evening the night itself was disguising her face.

* * *

Her voice alone should have made me suspicious. A magnificent gravelly voice, every inflexion etched by tobacco and corrosive drinking, a crumbling sandy wave crunching in the ear. And this voice came from a throat that had been eroded by time and from lips with creases at the corners. A lady.

Madame.

Her age? Fifty? Fifty-five? Perhaps sixty. But it was as if she had kept that face intact for years and years. The chauffeur headed straight for a smart building on the Avenue Victor-Hugo, and waited downstairs. Without

36

our exchanging a single word or so much as a look, I followed her up to the first floor and we went into an apartment that was smaller than I would have expected.

"Do sit down . . ."

Perhaps I would do well to call her "Madame" too. Had she been a very beautiful woman before now? Or had she become one after so many years?

"I won't try to keep you here, you know. He was so wild that I would never have guessed that he had a friend, a true friend."

Hearing the word "friend" I almost corrected her, but it would have been inappropriate and irrelevant.

"He often spoke about you."

"He did what?"

"You seem surprised . . . Antonio meant something to him. Antonio did well at school, Antonio did my homework for me, Antonio stopped me from doing lots of stupid things . . . If you had known each other as adults perhaps he wouldn't have . . ."

"He would have, all the same."

Without moving from the armchair I did a quick tour of the apartment. The little salon where they probably didn't spend much time, the two of them. A low table she would sling the keys onto. Not one cooking utensil, a fridge in one corner used only for ice cubes and for sparkling water, and its direct counterpart, a little further over, the bar, full of bottles of ochre and amber coloured liquids. And the bedroom, just opposite me, with the double bed where I could see it. An adjoining bathroom. Nothing that spoke of everyday life, but just the extras, the momentary, the parenthesis.

"We only came here to go to bed, if you want to know. Sometimes in the morning, frequently in the afternoon, as soon as I could, in fact."

"It's none of my business."

"We would come in, and usually he would take my clothes off in the hall, and we'd make love, he wouldn't let up for a moment. Then afterwards he would come and watch me take my shower."

"It's none of my business," I said again, embarrassed and avoiding her eye.

But I soon realized that she wanted neither to confide in me nor to shock me. She just wanted to talk about the fever they had known which was now lost, and about her body which was still capable of inflaming a dark, handsome boy in his thirties. She offered me a drink and a cigarette; seeing her efforts to be kind to me, I accepted the second.

"I recognized you straight away yesterday at the funeral. You're very like him, Antonio . . ."

"Physically?"

"Yes, of course, you have the same hair, you hold your head the same way, and you put your hands in your pockets when you're walking up stairs too. It's just your general appearance. But that's where it ends, Dario couldn't stay silent for more than ten seconds, he was untidy and ill-mannered, he never lived one minute without being obsessed about the next. He could ruin a moment's peace with just two words because he always had to be moving, because one day the world would recognize him. When he got carried away his Italian would come back to him in waves as he talked and I would lose track . . . He often used to say that one day there would be a miracle which . . ."

"What did he cost you?"

I had been burning to ask this question from the first moment I caught her eye. It's the sort of nasty question that should never be asked but I couldn't help it, eventually it just came out. If Madame

Raphaëlle has the wrinkles of a woman her age, she has the privileges too. She laughed.

"In money? I didn't keep count. The first time I saw him was at the dance hall, and I went back the next day, and every day, until we became more . . ."

"More intimate."

"If you like. At the time I paid, like all the others, and it was quite a price. Dario, good professional that he was, quickly grasped that I had a lot of money. When the owner of The Up offered him a job singing, I insisted that he accepted, and I even wanted to pay him the shortfall. I would have done anything to get him out of the clutches of all those . . ."

How could a woman like her have been dragged into something like this . . . Time on her hands. Boredom. Depravity. Playing with fire. Refusing to grow old. What else? How could Dario sell himself so readily? The crooner with his sentimental ballads, I still found that quite funny, but the mercenary gigolo was a bit much for me.

"I know what you're thinking . . . But the money wasn't a salary. To me, Dario wasn't a gigolo. Do you think he would have written me a letter like this if it had just been for the money?"

She took it out of her bag so that I could read it, and I pretended to look through it. It felt strange recognizing snatches of sentences that I'd turned and perfected in the discarded hull of a boat on a piece of wasteland. Now I couldn't tell whether it was Dario or myself who had written it, but Madame Raphaëlle was right, you don't write a letter like that to a customer you service while choking back your disgust.

Once again I looked right at her in all her astonishing beauty, the wrinkles in the corners of her eyes that she makes no effort to disguise, the grey hair she refuses to dye, and the same question came to me: has she always been beautiful or did she gradually become beautiful? But you definitely can't ask that sort of question.

"My husband is richer and more powerful than most people could imagine. There are at least four items in this room from his factories and everything else is from his wallet. We haven't spoken to each other for ten years but at my age you no longer want to risk your silence anywhere else."

"Did he ever know how you were connected to Dario?"

"No, impossible, he wouldn't have let me see him for fear of losing me."

She got up to pour herself another drink.

"Dario needed money. I have to accept the fact that at first he had every intention of getting a great deal out of me in a very short time. 140,000 francs to be precise."

How many afternoon trysts would it take to get that much together?

"For our first few rendezvous I played the game, two or three times, and then . . ."

And then, I didn't need to hear any more. Cupid aimed his final arrows and that old familiar tune began to play.

My poor Dario . . . When I think how fervently you chased after women when we were younger. We all wanted to see you settling down with a girl who would bear you the son that makes every Italian so proud. She would have cajoled you, you'd have made her laugh, you'd have built a house together. We'd all have come to celebrate. And your very last thoughts were for this woman, this dignified, refined French woman who was so far removed from the neighbourhood we grew up

40

in. I'm shocked, my friend. Shocked by this love that caught you unawares, at your age – and at her age. At what turned out to be the end of the road for both of you. The gigolo and the dowager.

"Antonio, I didn't come to find you so that I could talk about him for hours on end, but for a very particular reason. Do you know why he needed this money?"

She leant forward to pick up a sort of file from the coffee table by her feet. She opened it and laid out stacks of typed pages stapled together, all bearing seals and stamps that I couldn't begin to identify. "What you see before you is Dario's great dream . . ."

Hearing it described in those terms, I did everything I could to concentrate.

Contracts, official papers, but I hesitated for a moment in surprise when I realized they were all in Italian. Real Italian from over there with technical terms and plenty of pompous, sententious words, and I decided to wait for an explanation.

"You do understand, don't you?"

"No."

"These are property deeds. Ten acres of land in his native town. Weren't you born in Sora too . . .?"

She said this with a kindly smile, as if the name Sora would unleash in me a sort of gentle melancholy to the strains of a mandolin. What I felt about this return to the land was more like curiosity mingled with anxiety. Mamma Trengoni had mentioned this too but here now, despite the documents, I couldn't bring myself to imagine her crooner of a son going back to the motherland and putting on his boots to trudge through mud and shit in the hope of seeing anything grow one day. A taxi-boy dancer with his left hand on his heart and his right hand on a billhook. I'm

41

beginning to think that I really was the only person who knew Dario. He may have managed to reel in these women with his bucolic yearnings, but he would never have caught me out. He fooled the pair of them, no doubt about it.

"Did he want to build something? What is there on this land?"

"Vineyards. It's a little parcel of land between Sora and Santo Angelo. Did I pronounce that properly?"

"No, you have to elide it, Sant'Angelo, but it really doesn't matter because nobody gives a damn about him, the saint, I mean, and the locals only use his name to curse."

"I beg your pardon?"

"It's true, when they don't dare call on Christ or the Madonna, they abuse Sant'Angelo, it's not so serious. He's the scapegoat of the saints' calendar, his name punctuates every insult in the region. So, with or without the elision, no one gives a damn."

"Calm down . . ."

She put her hand on my knee. She looked at me intently but still didn't understand.

"You're so different from him . . . he felt so close to all this . . . he talked about it so . . . his land, his fellow countrymen, his name . . . And I think that's normal, don't you? With you it's as if the whole idea is positively painful. Usually, people who've come from another country are so . . ."

"You mean immigrants? Well, what about immigrants? What are they like?"

"They're . . . proud and vulnerable . . ."

A little laugh rose up and tickled my throat but I suppressed it quickly.

"And Dario suddenly became proud and powerful just by owning ten acres of vines?"

"He didn't get them just by clicking his fingers. The plot was divided between three different owners. He got five acres from his mother."

"Mamma Trengoni?"

"Are you surprised by that?"

No. Dario used to talk about his father's land as if they finally owned something worthwhile on this earth. Every wop has some vague plot of land they never got around to selling or getting enough out of it to pay their way and feed their bambini. My father's been banging on about some piece of woodland since forever, as if it were the great forest of Brocéliande. In fact, if my memory serves me right, it's a scraggy hump of land with a few scattered hazel trees where the shepherds sometimes go to get some shade. The old man has never tried to sell it, he knows that its value would scarcely cover the cost of getting there, paying a solicitor and eating the odd pizza. And at that price he's happier nurturing a hazy image in the back of his mind of his shady, wooded property. Not daft, my old man. And Dario's must have done the same sums.

"The remaining five acres were split between a man who's gone to live in the States, in New Jersey, and another who still lives in Italy, at Sant'Angelo. Did I get it right that time?"

"In New Jersey?"

"I paid for Dario's trip. The owner had actually forgotten about his little plot and he handed it over very readily for practically nothing. The hardest part was the Italian. He wanted to keep his bit for storing wood. Dario discussed it with him on site and managed to persuade him. By putting the three deeds together he became the owner of the whole vineyard. And that was it."

"I'm sure this is going to be a stupid question but what exactly did he want to do with this vineyard?"

"Make wine."

"Make what?"

"Wine."

This was the most improbable of answers.

"He wanted to leave France and go and make his wine, back there, and live off it. This was such a big plan, more important to him than anything else. More important than me. And when you love someone, especially at my age, that person's dreams always seem more real."

"That's impossible. Dario would never have worked the land. He knew absolutely nothing about making wine. Just try picturing him . . ."

"He would have learned, with time. Before Dario became the owner, one of the local peasants looked after the vines, and he never really made anything from them. I gave Dario enough money to take him on to tend the vines for the next three harvests, and the man agreed straight away. No one had wanted anything to do with that vineyard. It's almost as if it was just waiting for Dario to come and save it . . ."

She let herself drop down so that she was lying on the sofa, and she closed her eyes. My prying mind meant that I could now imagine them here together. Him with his arms in the air, twirling round the room talking about himself, himself, himself, about over there, about his dreams, and her, listening lovingly, drinking in her lover's infernal candour. I don't really have any intuition for that sort of thing, but I'm now quite sure that it was love. Even if there's a whiff of fraud hanging over it, a hint of the mercenary and of vested interest, none of this would have happened without a bit of unadulterated love. You'd have to be a

44

prude like me to be in any doubt and to pretend to be shocked.

"Antonio . . . I haven't told you the most important part. I don't know why Dario was taken from me. But I know that he's always harboured an incredible fear. A fear that this would all go wrong. He never talked to me about it, but he eventually put it in a letter. If anything happened to him, he wanted his land to go to the only people who had it in them to help him."

I lowered my eyes as I felt the ignition spark in my cardiac motor. And a strong urge to get out at great speed.

"Now, what would I be able to do with it, this piece of land? My life's here . . . Your country strikes me as so magnificent . . . It belongs to you. It's your land and I wouldn't know what to do with it."

I stood up.

"Dario knew that. He used to say that his mother would never go back to the old country and that, apart from me, all he had was . . ."

"Stop it!"

"He loved you, Antonio . . . Whether you like it or not . . . When he was with the solicitor he particularly wanted to add a name to the title deeds."

"Stop talking nonsense."

"If you refuse to take them, they'll be handed back to the community of Sora. But have them, it was his dying wish . . ."

"That's enough!"

The coffee table shifted as my foot accidentally knocked into it. She delved through the papers to prove that it was all written down, within the law, stamped and in order. My name, written out in full. What a nightmare.

"That's why I wanted to see you, Antonio. To give you these papers. And to fulfil his last wish."

Without really meaning to, I pushed past this woman who now stood blocking my way. When I read my name typed out on the page I nearly cried out in horror. Someone had power over me. I was being drawn in, imprisoned. Hounded.

"It was his last great dream, Antonio . . ."

I made a lunge for the door. She forced me to take the pile of papers.

And I fled, without a word, without trying to understand.

As far away as possible.

* * *

All my efforts to put as many miles and years as possible between myself and my childhood in the suburbs had evaporated in a few days. I really thought I'd extricated myself, like an ex-con who's decided to put it behind him, or a drug addict who's gone cold turkey. But no, the magnetic pull of the Rue Anselme-Rondenay is stronger than that, you can't get away whenever you want, perhaps that was what Dario meant when he said the road is long. I would have to change my name, dye my hair blond, leave France, and start all over again, somewhere else, as an immigrant, back in the vicious circle. I'm going to have to pay a high price if the Italian community is to forget me. I always refused to set foot on my ancestors' land and now a plot of it belongs to me by right. How can I fail to interpret this as proof that there is a cynical god? Not to mention Dario's ghost clinging to me even more than he did when we used to drag our feet up and down the streets together.

Two o'clock in the morning. In the rooms opposite I can see the party's still in full swing. I open the window wide to try and get some air. If I do manage to get to sleep I can tell I'm going to dream about him.

Dario . . . you're a real bastard. You'd already put my name next to yours on those bits of paper from the solicitor long before you got me to write that letter. You were happier insulting me than admitting something like that to me. Admitting that you still thought of me as a friend. And you knew that it hadn't been reciprocal for a long time. Now that I think about it, I wonder whether the letter really was addressed to Madame Raphaëlle. Perhaps you were even more Machiavellian than that. Perhaps you were actually writing it to me when you made me translate it. Bastard. You should have told me about this wine. Wine . . .? How could someone as lazy as you ever grow wine? You've never even tasted it. I've always heard that the wine from Sant'Angelo is so bad it's scary, even my father wouldn't want it. I can't see why you sold first your body and then your soul for some plonk that's given everyone in the region heartburn. Was it that you wanted to make it drinkable at last, and to succeed where everyone else had failed? Or did you feel the call of your native land rippling through you, did you tell yourself it was your paradise lost, and that there was still time to catch up on all those years?

Pointless conjecturing. Dario would never have got involved in such a dead-end project. There's something dodgy about this plot of land and it's not just the grapes. Dodgy or lined with gold. I miss my father already. He's the only person who could have told me about this parcel of land where he used to take his turkeys to feed. He could have told me about the land and the wine, put together all the anecdotes and in amongst them I would have found a clue, an idea. In every village there are rows that go back generations between clans wielding shotguns and squabbling over concessions till the end of time, but what's the link with a badly employed Franco-Italian who looks as much like a landowner as Frank Sinatra looks like a verger running late for the angelus.

I sat down at my desk to read through the documents carefully, and I even took out my French–Italian dictionary just in case.

First, the names of the former owners.

Giuseppe Parini, Trenton, New Jersey, U.S.A. Two and a half acres. North-North-East, sold for nine million five hundred thousand lira.

Let's call that fifty thousand francs. In other words, a gift.

Mario Mangini Sant'Angelo, Lazio, Italy Two and a half acres. South. Eighteen million lira.

The Italian asked nearly twice as much. With the five acres old Mother Trengoni had graciously handed over, that makes a respectable ten-acre vineyard acquired for a song. The papers mention a cellar, a barn and a tool shed. The whole lot generously given by a woman in love who didn't hesitate before quietly drawing on her husband's funds.

I suddenly found the whole masquerade maddening, as if I could feel Dario manipulating me from beyond the grave, and I swept my arm across the desk, throwing the whole lot to the floor. My model almost fell down with it. I switched on all the lights in my studio. My cheeks were flushed with the early July heat.

All of a sudden I heard a muffled sound and at the same time I felt a burning sensation on my neck. I didn't even understand what it was straight away.

Surprised, I dodged down onto my knees with my head under the table. I put my hand up to the nape of my neck and my fingers slipped cloyingly down to my shoulder. Without really knowing why, I flattened myself on the ground like an obedient corpse already beginning to sag, when I actually felt I'd scarcely been touched. Intrigued and out of harm's way as I crouched under my chair with my hand clamped round my neck, I tried to understand what was going on. Two or three images flitted through my mind in a split second, hornets in summer humming just before they sting, the hot invisible slice of a razor, a badly healed wound secretly oozing. Lying there prostrate and incredulous, I listened out for complete silence, then turned to look at the open window. All I saw were a few scattered stars and, much lower down, the halo of orange light coming from the building opposite. A hazy sound, distant clinking, voices intermingling and perhaps, in the background, a hint of volatile music. As I crawled over to the bathroom I saw that my neck was leaving a trail of red droplets and then, finally coming back to reality, I felt afraid. Afraid that I would empty myself of all my blood, that in the blinking of an eye I would be drowning in a great flow of blood; it's easy to imagine this torrent and then nothing. I struggled to stay conscious until I'd staunched the bleeding firstly with a towel and then, after knocking over all the shelves, with a long strip of cotton wool which far too quickly became drenched in my precious blood. I waited a long time before looking at myself in the mirror, with a deep-seated conviction that this source would never run dry. Whatever sort of vein can there be in the nape of the neck to piss out blood like this, I thought. And it started to slow down. Even though I didn't dare take off the cotton wool I could feel that the stream had abated, that there was still enough juice in me to stay conscious. With the bottle of pure alcohol in my hand, I hesitated a long time before sloshing it haphazardly over the gash. The martyred screams that this produced from me did nothing to compensate for the stupidity of the action.

On the terrace opposite the cocktail party's coming to an end, a couple of party goers gaze at the stars, still laughing a little. A waiter switches off the lights and clears away the last few glasses. Four floors below a cohort of well-oiled characters share a few more bursts of laughter before spreading out towards their cars. The whole thing's a bit like an end of year party from some computer company, complete with optimistic speech from the managing director, and statutory jokes from the rather drunk minions. Keeping a towel wrapped round my neck like a scarf, I've searched all round the chair I was sitting in ten minutes earlier. The bullet that grazed me is buried in the wall. I found a second impact in the wooden upright of the book-shelves. At the moment I can't see any more and that tallies with the noises I heard. No loud bangs. A clear sight-line from the terrace. Even though I don't have the first idea about ballistics I can guess that the bullets must have been fired from over there, from amongst the party-goers.

I hurried down the stairs with the unpleasant impression that the haemorrhaging would start again. Leaning up against my sister's car, I spotted two night owls kissing passionately. The girl was frightened when she saw my sweat-stained face wrapped in a bloody towel, and I didn't have to ask twice for them to move on. Jumping a few red lights I got to the Fifteenth Arrondissement and I headed down the Rue de la

Convention, driving like a condemned man. I tried not to swallow, cough or even move my head, convinced that the wound only needed the slightest movement to open again. Once there, I woke a friend of mine who's a nurse and who didn't ask too many questions about how I got the injury. Given the state I was in, the first thing she did was to give me a pill, without actually telling me it was a tranquillizer. She dressed it again, swearing that stitches would be pointless. On the way home I sat meekly harnessed by my seat belt and drove no faster than 30mph. As if I'd finally grasped the fact that I was still alive. I parked in front of the building opposite my apartment, and went up the stairs to the Salons Laroche, not bothering to wait for the lift. The last three waiters tried to stop me going out onto the balcony.

"What the hell difference does it make to you, your stupid party's finished, hasn't it? And you let anybody in here, don't you? Anyone can walk past and see the lights, and they get in straight away. Anybody can, I'd put money on it. Sooner or later I bet you let a killer through those doors!"

They were so dumbfounded they didn't try to stop me for long. From up on the terrace I could see my desk with the light still on, as well as a good deal of the rest of the room. It even felt close enough to jump over the road to get back there. Two minutes later I'd pulled the blinds down and collapsed on the bed.

You didn't have to be a genius to realize the vineyard was cursed. Dario didn't last long and I nearly died after I'd only had it for a couple of hours. Whoever comes into possession of those few acres is condemned to death. You could say that this just endorses my doubts about Dario's, shall we say, agricultural voca-tion. There's much more at stake than Madame

Raphaëlle's prepared to believe, and Dario had sniffed out something juicy about this little plot otherwise he wouldn't have prostituted himself in order to get hold of it in such a hurry. The big hurry for me was to get rid of it as quickly as possible. That bastard Dario didn't leave me the instructions manual. He already knew there was a trap. Thanks for the present. I'm not ready to die for this. Someone's looking for me. Probably whoever killed Dario. He could be anywhere, outside, on the corner of the street. He could be waiting for me outside my front door. He might be there now. And the worst of it is that for now, until I've untangled this muddle, I'm going to have to get out of Paris.

*   *   *

Porte de Choisy. As I went over the Périphérique ring road I felt like I was ploughing my way into a great block of misery and boredom. I'd have liked to close my eyes so that I didn't have to watch those four miles unfolding, four miles of a perpetually undulating ribbon that lay between me and the Rue Anselme-Rondenay.

God, you suburbs are depressing. You've got nothing going for you. There you are with your eyes turned towards Paris and your arse towards the countryside. You can only ever be a compromise. You're boredom incarnate. But what I resent most about you is that you stink of work. All you care about is the morning, and you set your curfew the minute everyone comes out of the factories. People take their bearings from your chimneys. I've never heard anyone say they minded leaving you behind. You've never had time to create your own kind of well-being. You're not old and you've never had patience, you always want more of everything, and bigger, you've got plenty of room for all the megastores and hypermarkets. The only thing that changes with you is the lunacy of the architects. They give me a living with their models intended for you. Your infernal mosaic. They're having a ball with you, you're their bacchanal, their orgy, their bulimia. They gorge themselves on all this space, a futuristic enclave here, right next to the urban development zone, next to the gaudy coloured gymnasium, between the nondescript 1950s' district just waiting to be re-developed and a shopping mall that's changed name twenty times. If, by chance, a marauding motorway fly-over hasn't carved its way over the lot. You're quite right not to give a damn about harmonious lines because you've never had any and you never will. So let them get on with it, all of them with their avant-garde ideas, with their visionary use of breeze blocks, they make you feel as if you're being reborn when, in fact, you'll never die. You'll just stretch out a bit further, you'll eat up more space around you but you'll never turn up your toes. And that's the only true thing about you. You can't be disfigured, you've never had a face.

I took my mother by surprise, singing to herself as she cooked the carbonara. We had lunch together, just the two of us, with no TV or tomato sauce, no wine and hardly any conversation. My mother could have made being single her life's work. I liked seeing her like that, miles from everything, enjoying her solitude, not suspecting for one moment what I was going through.

"Why've you got that bandage on your neck?"

"I had a sort of stiff neck. How do you say stiff neck in Italian?"

"*Torticollo*. You're father's been sending us postcards."

54

An aerial view of Perros-Guirec. Another showing the thermal springs. The same as last year. He doesn't say anything, or hardly. He seems happy.

I quickly changed the subject by asking her how she'd been spending her free time since her husband had left. She goes to see Mamma Trengoni, sitting for minutes at a time without saying a word, then she tries to get her to get out for some fresh air but doesn't always succeed. The policemen haven't shown up again, and the local gossips have already stopped chuntering on about Dario's death. Everything seems to be going back to normal.

"Have some more parmesan, Antonio. It goes well with carbonara."

She'll do anything to avoid being lumbered with a tomato sauce. As soon as her husband's out of sight she uses the opportunity to do something different, like today. Egg, parmesan, bacon pieces, all mixed up with the spaghetti. Quick and delicious.

"Do you know why it's called carbonara?" I ask.

"Because you should always add pepper at the last minute, and the black on the white looks like coal dust, and even the fried bacon looks a bit like little lumps of coal."

She smiles. I think she's wrong but I don't want to disabuse her. It actually comes from the Carbonari who formed secret societies in the woods. Good conspirators that they were, they invented this recipe specially so that their meetings didn't drag on for ever. But she doesn't know the first thing about secrets or conspiracies.

She glanced at the clock and said that the telephone would ring, and ring it did. She picked up the receiver unhurriedly. My old man on the other end would never have guessed that I was listening in on the earpiece. He seemed to have rediscovered a serenity he'd lost. In fact, after forty years of marriage, it does him just as much good as my mother to spend a bit of time on his own, with his friends. I asked him in passing whether he knew the wine from Sant'Angelo.

"Why do you ask, have you had some, my son? As soon as I go away you have to go and do something stupid . . ."

He burst out laughing but I didn't join him, I forced myself to chat for a bit longer and then I hung up.

For five or six days I covered the whole neighbourhood, looking for bits and bobs of things, impressions, information, memories. I went round all my old friends, the sons of Sora and Sant'Angelo, I chatted for a while with the parents, sometimes even the occasional grandparent. Some told me about the vineyard, and about the legend of Sant'Angelo which had been told down the generations. Sora is a godforsaken place with three distinguishing features: firstly, weird shoes made from discarded lorry tyres and laced like Roman sandals. Secondly, in the late eighteenth century, the apparition of a saint who then became the patron saint of the vineyard. Thirdly, from 1945 onwards, the wholesale emigration of all the able-bodied men who came home from the war. My father was amongst them, as were almost all the others who had come to settle in Vitry. The Cuzzo family told me about their American cousin, Giuseppe Parini, who'd owned two and a half acres of the vineyard. Nothing to say, except that he'd forgotten all about Europe and didn't give a fig what when on there. He owned two or three factories and a chain of fast-food outlets, and he was already plenty busy enough with the Italians over there. That said it all. I didn't feel like digging further. Mamma Trengoni let me go into Dario's bedroom where I found nothing except for a rather fuzzy photograph of Madame Raphaëlle, well hidden in the sleeve of an old forty-five record.

I came across Osvaldo laying the first bricks of his palace, his edifice, his Xanadu. His own personal bungalow. We chatted for a while. He was putting his heart into it. All on his own. Helped along by the watchful eyes of his son who was barely three. And he was waiting to see *la casa* too. I only hope Osvaldo will really create a little place of his own, somewhere between the kitchen, the sitting room and the children's bedrooms. Because, what with celebrating mothers and celebrating children, Italian fathers tend to forget about themselves a bit, despite their loud mouths. I wished him good luck with his work, it was the best I could come up with.

I slept in my parents' house, and it felt odd going back to that old bed in that old room with the old light on the bedside table, and the old TV no one ever said I couldn't watch. One thing was sure, whoever had it in for me the other night hadn't followed me all the way out here. You could be forgiven for thinking that even killers are frightened of the suburbs. I'm beginning to understand what Dario meant by "My road is long." He was probably talking about the Italian diaspora that took refuge wherever you could put a roof over your head, without sparing any corner of the universe. Just within the Rue Anselme-Rondenay I inventoried direct connections with three continents. All you have to do is talk to some guy who has a brother whose best friend has moved to such and such a place where you might end up one day, if you felt like it. Dario knew that. He could have raised cattle on a ranch in Australia, or repainted the walls of Buenos Aires, or sold cheese in London, worked in the mines of Lorraine or set up his own cleaning company in Chicago. Until anything better came along, he'd opted for being a gigolo in Paris.

Better. But what was it? Now I know that that's for me to find out.

I made my decision a while ago, actually. I have to know what he saw in that parcel of land. That's probably the price I'll have to pay if I ever want to feel free. If I want to understand what my father will always hide from me. This is a score I have to settle with my native land. My scale models can wait another month. I've already been forced to leave Paris. Tomorrow I'll leave France.

But at least I'll know.

Before leaving I asked my mother whether she'd like it if I went back to Sora.

"To live?" she asked, surprised.

"Yes."

She said nothing for a long time, speechless after such an unexpected question. I even thought she might be annoyed.

"To do what? We're here now ... there's no one from our family back there now ... you're French. You're not going to start the whole business all over again with the travelling, looking for a house, getting your papers and looking for a girlfriend over there, and work and getting on with the neighbours, and everything ... Even the language you speak, they're not going to understand you. Stay here, go on. I certainly don't want to go back there, not even for a holiday."

The next day I left her to her blissful ignorance.

* * *

The Palatino, departing at 18.06, the most famous of the Paris–Rome trains and something of an institution to the wops, at least to those who've elected to live around the Gare de Lyon. They talk about it as if it were a weary old horse which always ends up coming home. The last time I used it was way back when I was eleven or twelve. I found the outward journey unbearably long and the homeward journey even worse.

"What time do we get to Rome?" I ask.

The young guy in the blue blazer with a sleeper badge on his lapel is short, dark-haired, a bit scruffy and permanently grumpy. He looks at me with the exasperation of someone who has to keep saying the same thing over and over again.

"At 10.06, if the Italians don't make us late."

"Do they sometimes?"

At this he just sniggers without giving a reply.

"It must be fun working on the night trains, isn't it?" I ask him.

"When you've been four times round the world by train we'll talk again, okay?"

He goes out of the compartment with a shrug.

There are five of us, an Italian couple on their way home from their honeymoon, a French couple going to Rome on holiday for the first time, and me. My travelling companions are charming, both couples making themselves understood with gestures and smiles, and a few tentative sentences that their opposite numbers always manage to understand. There's the occasional word that brings them up short, but I wouldn't contemplate filling in the gaps for them, that would do me out of some of my fun. Every now and then I fall asleep, rocked by the train, and I forget that I've left behind the country and the city that I love. For an indefinite period. I convince myself that it's no big deal, a picnic compared to what my father and grand-father had to live through. Exile is an unhealthy obsession with Italians. I can't see why I should be the exception to the rule. Childhood memories come back to me. Memories of all the departures I haven't experienced. My father's voice surges back, like those evenings when he happened to feel like talking about himself.

. . . Going away . . . ? Before I was even born my father set off for America to try and bring home some dollars. Then it was my brothers. When it was my turn we'd got to 1939, and I left anyway, but not to make my fortune, just to learn how to carry a rifle on military service. It was in Bergamo, in the North, with people talking in every dialect under the sun. Luckily I found a guy from my region to talk to in secret, because we were forbidden to talk in patois. We became compari, *and that was a word that really meant something, like a promise of friendship. And in the evenings we would traipse through the mountain town, my* compare *and me, and we would watch the fascist troops coming to blows with the Mountain Infantry, with their feathers in their hats. They were the only ones who stood up to Mussolini's guys. Everything was free for the black shirts, they would go into a cinema or a bar and say "The Duce's paying!" That's probably what made me hate those bastards right from the start . . . and that was nothing compared to the war itself, the real war. In '41 they wouldn't even give me time to go home and see my fiancée. They sent us away, my* compare *and me . . . you'll never guess where . . . to a country we didn't even know existed . . . That's when I really understood what it meant to go away . . .*

Someone's shaking me by the shoulder. 10.34. Roma Termini. Even before I get off the train I can feel something, I don't know what yet, a summer heat, a strange smell, a smell of summer heat, a really white quality to the light, I don't know. Bustle on the platform. From my vantage point on the running board, I look at all those arms criss-crossing backwards and forwards; the handrail is almost burning, the green hull of the train opposite shines in the sunlight. I make my way up the platform. In the distance the station concourse looks almost grey in the shadow of the great glass canopy. It looks like a perfectly rectangular aquarium, huge and rather dirty, thronging and buzzing with overweight, agitated and already sweating tourists. This is still an illicit free zone, pandemonium. After changing some money I make up my mind to get out of the aquarium. To my left and my right there are two great vaults of light and I don't know which way to go to launch myself once and for all into this country.

I choose the left-hand exit, it's the nearest, the one everyone always takes given that it leads out to the bus terminal on the via dei Mille. I stand motionless on the threshold of the station, not quite daring to cross the road. That's Rome right there, on the pavement opposite, I recognize it even though I've never really known it. Walls of ageing ochre, the tram tracks, a Caffè Trombetta with two old men sitting at a table with their feet in the sun and their heads tilted towards the shade from the blind, fidgety little cars piling past each other in a colloquial exchange of tootings. I tell myself I've got to move on. To reach the coaches I walk along the Via Principe Amadeo and I'm fascinated by everything, scrutinizing every last little stall to see whether it corresponds with the vague memories I still have. A barber with no customers lying back in one of his chairs in the shampooing position, reading his paper in the half light. I pass two gypsies, two *zingare*, who hold out their hands to me. Under a sign that says

61

Pizza & Pollo there are workmen eating chicken thighs as they argue in a dialect not far removed from the one my parents use, but I pass them too quickly to grasp the contention. I cross the street, onto the sunny side. I can see a long row of coaches in the distance. Mine leaves at eleven, I've still got a bit of time. There are families laden with bags and children grouped round the sign for departures to Sora. "*Dieci minuti! Dieci minuti, no c'è furia! Non c'è furia!*" the driver calls to the mob that keeps trying to get into his vehicle. Opposite the terminal I see another barber who has just as little work as the first. I run my hand over my stubble.

He looks up at me. The moment has come, now I'll see whether I can put them off the track and avoid being taken for a tourist. His Italian is crystalline. Not a whiff of accent.

"For a shave or a haircut, *signore*?"

"A shave."

"When does your bus leave?"

"In ten minutes."

"That's fine."

It would seem I've coped quite well with the first words I've spoken in this transalpine land, with a bit of luck he won't even have noticed I'm French. He rubs a warm towel over my face, sharpens his razor and daubs my chin with foam. The blade makes a squeaking sound over my cheek. It's the first time I've been shaved by someone else. It's nice. Except when he goes right down to my Adam's apple. It's warm and very precise.

A gust of wind suddenly blows in, a draught which slams the door shut and makes a pile of magazines on the side of the basin fall to the ground. The blade doesn't deviate by one millimetre.

Phlegmatic, steady, all he says is: "*Per bacco . . . Ché vento impetuoso!*" By Bacchus, what an impetuous wind! I'll never get used to their turn of phrase in this country.

Two minutes later my skin is smoother than glass. The barber smiles at me and asks me sneakily:

"So, are you from Paris or Haÿ-les-Roses?"

Trying to hide my disappointment, I tell him Paris. He must have some distant cousin in the Second Arrondissement.

I pay, ashamed to have been found out. I don't know how long I'm going to stay here, but it would've been better if they'd taken me for a real native. Before leaving the barber's shop, the barber gratifies me with an "*au revoir*" in an exaggeratedly heavy accent, just to point out that he's travelled too. Back outside, the mob has disappeared from round the sign, and the windows on the bus are fugging up. There's one fold-away seat left next to the driver. He sets off, streaming with sweat, and winks at me as he says "If you look out now, you will see the Coliseum!" in the same heavily accented French as the barber.

So, there it was. And after the Coliseum, the country-side. The old crate went through tiny village after tiny village, gradually dropping off all those who'd been on the same Palatino as myself, and picking up locals, women with huge baskets, children coming home from school. The whole enterprise ringing with a cheerful cacophony of conversation as people swapped places, doing the rounds of everyone they knew as if the whole village was gathered in that bus. One woman just behind me shrieked with laughter as she told some farmyard anecdote which commanded virtually everyone's attention for the last six miles. I

63

laughed too, although I didn't really understand, and I began to wonder what would have happened if my father hadn't decided to leave the area. My mother could have been that woman with the copper coloured neck, the expansive gestures and the contagious laugh. And I could have been the young lad in the yellow vest reading *La corriere dello sport* and twiddling a toothpick in his mouth, completely oblivious to the pandemonium around him. After all, why not? At this very moment my father would be out in his forest overseeing the youngsters at work, waiting for his plateful of macaroni. On the other hand I can't for a minute see myself wearing a woollen singlet, I don't like football and I've always thought toothpicks were rather vulgar.

I got out at the end of the line, at Sora. Sant'Angelo is a little dependent hamlet which lies two miles to the north. The only memory I have of Sora is a river called the Liri, four bridges that cross over it and three cinemas, which, at the time, showed different films every day. With fewer inhabitants than there were seats available. You could smoke in the balcony, but there was a sign forbidding customers from eating pizza. One of the auditoria was like a big Rex cinema, another specialized in B-movie epics, and the smaller, third one in porn and horror films. I remember one screening of *The Plucky Niece* when the projectionist was nearly lynched by the hysterical audience: the lights had failed just as the niece in question was about to demonstrate all her pluck when confronted by a great burly bully who was making her choose between his member and his axe. We never did find out what happened. When I went back to France I couldn't find enough words to explain to my friends what the human race was capable of doing up on the big screen.

Only Dario could corroborate what I said. Cinema was a part of day-to-day life for the little Italian provincial, for the peasant in fact. Now all I can see are dishes on all the roofs; the three cinemas have disappeared. The largest has become a garden machinery shop, and I wonder what the local kids have to do now to get a taste of forbidden images.

It's already too hot. My bag weighs a ton. I'm wearing what I would be wearing in Paris, and people are seeing me as a tourist without really knowing what's different about me. It's written all over my face. I can read it in theirs. The town is nicer than I remembered it. More variety in the colours of the walls, in the architecture, in the way the little shops and stalls are set up. I hadn't taken all that in as a child. Children never notice anything, except for ice-cream stalls and cinemas. I'm sweating. I'm hungry. I can smell warm flour wafting from a pizzeria. Right next to it, a smell of brine. Mountains of yellow olives. And on the Piazza Santa Restituta the man who sells watermelons is unloading his lorry by rolling the fruit down a wide plank of wood. Feeling a bit bewildered, I can't make a decision, can't decide whether to eat, drink, sleep or to leave straight away and go back where I have come from, so I sit down next to an ornamental pond, completely alone. No one dares confront the sun yet.

Pensione Quadrini. They told me I'd find a room there. A covered porch which opens onto a minute patio cluttered with rusting bicycles and a moped. A small, dark staircase leads straight into a kitchen where a young woman is frying courgette flowers without taking her eyes off the television. She wipes her hands on her apron and, surprised, asks me what I want. As if I'd come to eat her flower fritters. A room? Oh yes, a room! I have four . . . four rooms! That's all I can make out. Despite her enthusiasm I sense she's uncomfortable, she blushes and won't look me in the eye. We're swamped by the smell of frying, and she isn't used to tourists. Makes you wonder who it is she puts up here right in the middle of August. In fact, everything happens quite quickly. There isn't even time to talk. It's as if she wants to get it over with. It wouldn't take much for me to turn on my heel. No desire to disturb someone's peace and quiet on my very first day. I follow her into a little room which is very basic but clean, with a missal on the bedside table and a pious picture above the bed. Signorina Quadrini puts a towel by the basin and says something about hot water (there isn't any at certain times of day), then she rummages through a pocket in her apron to give me my key, in case I come in after eleven o'clock at night. I think she is going to discuss the rates and the length of my stay but, still looking rather anxious, she goes back to her kitchen to get on with her frying.

What is this strange place I've landed in? Are the real wops different from us, the renegades?

The bed creaks as much as my poor body which is still stiff from my night in a couchette. No one knows I'm in this godforsaken place. I'm not even really sure of it myself. I'm going to have to get used to all this if I'm going to understand anything.

The property deeds are spread out on the floor and I'm studying them for the hundredth time. Extracts from the land registry, the surveyor's map, and my name, my name, and my name again. It's because of these three pieces of paper that Dario is dead and that I myself have come so close to finishing up in the Cimetière du Progrès. I've had a mental picture of my land for several days, and now that I'm so close to it, a stone's throw away, I still recoil each time I think I've gathered enough courage to go there. The 900 miles from Paris to Rome are nothing compared to this. On the edge of my land. My land. Sometimes I do manage to accept it, to appropriate it, to behave as if I have some pride in it. When all I really feel is fear and contempt.

Mediterranean reflexes come back quickly. After a brief siesta, I go out at about six o'clock in the evening, the best part of the day. That's when people dare to venture out, when they feel like mixing with each other, chatting in public places, out on terraces, with a glass of nice, chilled red wine in their hands. They can tolerate the feeling of a shirt on their skin, they no longer hesitate before making the least move, they stroll up and down. I drink a cup of coffee right in front of the little pond where all the younger generation have gathered. The girls are sitting on the sides being hassled by boys on mopeds. There are men eating ice-creams. None of this is very different from what I knew as a boy. I feel less of an intruder than when I first arrived.

Acting on a sudden impulse, I started walking along the verge of the road to Sant'Angelo. I had a strong urge to go there, as if all my courage had come back and everything was going to become clear at last. As I walked I went back over all the theories about my plot of land. But there were more than a hundred. More than a thousand.

There is something hidden under this land, something buried, some treasure, millions, gold, precious objects, gold ingots that date back to the war, the holy grail, the bodies of thirty people who've disappeared, irrefutable proof of guilt on loads of crimes, things that would be better left undisclosed. That's why I nearly ended up being killed.

But if there really is something buried here, what is wrong with one simple nocturnal expedition with a pick and shovel, and be done with it. Unless it is too big to dig up discreetly. Anything is possible. And if there really is something, then that something is mine by right. I could be a millionaire without knowing it. And what the hell do I care if it's cost me a nine-millimetre bullet in the head?

Just a few more yards. With the map from the land registry in my hand, I leave the road and head into a small wood. It's cooler, I breathe in the unfamiliar smells, skirt round bushes with strange-looking berries. My heart starts beating faster. Between two oak trees I see a sort of clearing in the distance that could well belong to me. The sun is still high in the sky. I haven't seen a living soul for a good half hour.

This is it all right.

Tidy. Modest. Not stretching for miles, no, I can see the boundaries and the contours of it by just moving my head slightly. It stops at the foot of the hill. The stakes are good and upright, the bunches of fruit visible, though still green. A sort of old barn not far away. And of course no suggestion of a boundary to hem it all in. After all, who gives a damn about these ten unfenced little acres? You can see the full extent of them at a glance, and you could walk round the perimeter in no time. You'd hardly notice it if you hadn't come specially to see it. It's surrounded by a much bigger field of corn. How many men would it take to look after it? Two, three at the most, and not every day. Three days here, ten days there. No more. I go over to the barn, being careful not to tread on the cultivated earth, as if I'm more worried about the mud itself than my shoes. The barn isn't even locked. It's used for storing the pressing equipment and a few barrels which are clearly empty. Is this wine really as bad as they say it is? How can you make bad wine with countryside and sunshine like this? And why's no one ever tried to improve it, to make something a bit more drinkable out of it? Because, apparently, with a bit of goodwill, a bit of enthusiasm, a bit of science and a bit of money you can turn vinegar into something more than acceptable. I feel like an intruder, like someone the local peasants will want to see off with their rifles, and hand over to the Carabinieri. When, in fact, I'm well and truly on my own property, and I've got all the papers to prove it. Once inside the barn I see a great pile of straw and in the middle of it a corked cask which reeks of cheap wine and looks full to bursting. I don't know how to go about getting a mouthful of it without spilling several pints of the stuff all over the floor. There's a ladle nearby, a hammer and a big flat stone. I'll have to put the cask upright but it must weigh a good hundredweight.

Just as I am going over towards it I hear a rasping breath from beyond the grave.

The scream seems to echo everywhere, and I am terrified, I scrabble like a rat, retracing my steps. The scream is repeated a couple of times and then becomes a hoarse groan. Scarcely human. But I do manage to recognize a couple of words.

"*Chi é!!! Chi é? Chi é?*"

If this whatever it is is asking who I am, then it can't really be dangerous. I go back over to the cask and that's when I see his round, podgy face, streaming with wine, wearing thick round glasses with black lenses, and I make out his chubby body under the straw. He's lying amongst the empty demijohns. One of them is lying down next to him, still a quarter full, just where he can reach it with his mouth. He was suckling from it when I came and disturbed him. I try to catch his eye but his strange black glasses are impenetrable; he makes a vague effort to sit up but doesn't get to his feet. He has long hair, a dirty beard, a filthy jacket and clumpy old shoes full of holes. I would never have guessed that there would be tramps here. He tries a few failed movements, like getting to his feet, picking up something that is hidden in the straw, but mostly just looks in my direction. I realize that he is blind drunk. His knees knock into whatever it is that is buried and I hear a few tuneless twanging sounds. He bursts out laughing and fumbles through the straw to find the thing that has made the noise. A banjo. He lays it on his knee and looks over towards me with his mouth gaping open, apparently happy. The smile of a contented man, laughing into the sad and bewildering abyss. But I have the peculiar impression that his eyes are ten feet wide of their mark.

"My name is Antonio Polsinelli."

"Never heard of him, *signore*. But that doesn't matter! In fact, it's a good thing! Are you just visiting?"

"Yes."

"Well, that's very good!"

He strums the strings by way of an introduction and says: "You won't ever have heard this, I'm going to play you a song that I've written myself, the song of my whole life, it's a lament, it's sad, it's called 'I Bought Every Colour'."

By shaking the cask he manages to drink a few mouthfuls and to spill several pints on the floor. Then he starts to sing his song.

> *The fields of corn are black*
> *The sky is black in the day and in the night again*
> *How sad, how sad to see only in black*

The wind, the sun and the rain.
Went to the market to find some colour
But the stallholder said, "You'll need money for that!"
What colour is money? I don't even know that
One day a man came, he was black too
He told me that soon I would see everything in gold
I expected a rainbow, I wanted millions
But he died before he was old
And I console myself playing my tune
And the kind passers-by throw me coins
And to forget all the black that's always mine
Went to the market to buy some red wine
"I have no more red," the man said to me
"You'll have to drink white." And he added with glee
"What difference can it make to a blind man like you
If the bottle is in a different hue?"

A shot rang out in the barn and I screamed in surprise again. The blind man fell silent. Kneeling stiffly. I thought he'd been shot.

A figure was silhouetted, standing squarely by the door with the gun still in the air. The blind man and I stood frozen, helpless. The man came over slowly and in an incredible paroxysm of anger he hit the blind man in the ribs with the butt of his rifle. Gasp of pain. I didn't move an inch.

Fear of violence, of gunshots, of everything, this country, the blind man and his song, this man taking pleasure from beating a poor handicapped creature sprawling on the ground.

Insults, kicks. I loathed myself for not knowing how to stop it.

Then he hurled the blind man out of the barn and threw the banjo as far away as he could. He snapped a long stick, which must have been used as a walking

71

stick, over his knee. Then he turned calmly towards me with a chilling smile.

"Is sir the new owner of the land?"

His Italian was refined, a little too academic, too deliberate. Rather like my father on an important day. And that polite, deferential use of the third person was a little too precious, something you would only use to address someone older as a mark of respect. Having momentarily lost my voice, I lowered my arms, not knowing what to say, not really knowing whether he was speaking to me or to someone else hidden behind me.

"The blind man isn't a bad old boy, but I've tried to get him off this vineyard a thousand times. He keeps knocking over the barrels, and Giacomo who tends the vine can't be here every day to oversee things."

"You shouldn't have beaten him like that."

"Pfff . . . If I hadn't he would have been back within a couple of hours."

"So?"

He twitches, irritated by my reaction. A real *padrone*, as he would call him, would know how to command respect. Then he resumes his unbearable smile.

"Sir must make his presence felt straight away, or he will have nothing but trouble. The blind man knows me well, it's all right . . . I give him 1,000 lira at the market on Sundays . . . if everyone listened to what the blind man had to say . . ."

"Who are you?"

"Signor Mangini Mario. I live next door. I sold a plot of land which now belongs to sir."

He extends his hand towards me. Still under the effects of shock, I reach mine to him.

"Did sir know him well, the dead man, Mr Polsinelli?"

"You know everything, don't you? Even my name."

He launched into a little explanatory spiel, which didn't reveal any surprises. Dario had travelled down from Paris to pay cash for a little parcel of land he no longer needed. They didn't discuss the price for long and went straight to the solicitor. It was the same solicitor who'd been contacted by telephone – probably by Madame Raphaëlle – to say that the deeds of the property would be in a different name following Dario's death, and the news circulated amongst those with an interest in the land. Mangini ended his speech saying that sooner or later he knew he would eventually meet the "new owner".

"Dario must have explained why he wanted to buy it?" I asked.

He sniggered.

"I tried to understand, at first. Because you know, Signor Polsinelli, even an old man of the land like myself, born and bred here, would never be able to make anything of this vineyard, so ... with all due respect to the dead, I can safely say that some little Frenchman wasn't going to turn the place into something special ..."

He says this with that little note of pride of the invincible native, a man who's never left his native soil or stooped so low as to ask for help from another country. There's probably some sort of honour in not running away from all this. I don't know. During this lull in the conversation he slings his gun over his shoulder and stands bolt upright, like a soldier standing to attention. I try to guess his age, but can't really pinpoint it. Haughty bearing, precise movements, an unusual display of strength when he was beating up the blind man. Lots of wrinkles, his face tanned by the sun, a weary expression. Sixty, maybe.

"Polsinelli, that's an Italian name. And sir speaks it well, almost like us. How come?"

"My parents are from round here."

"I thought that might be the case . . . there are quite a few Polsinellis here . . . it's like me, there are masses of Manginis, from at least three different families . . . Do you know what they say about Italy? That it's the country of sculptors, painters, architects, uncles, nephews and cousins . . ."

We're heading back out of the barn. The sun has set rapidly, unless our conversation has gone on longer than I think. Once outside, Mangini points out the boundaries of the property with a panoramic sweep of his arm.

"And the little building that sir can see over there, that's where the tools are kept, I wouldn't recommend even going in there, it's so old it could fall down on top of sir. There's nothing in there that's worth anything. Not enough to buy a packet of cigarettes."

When I glance over towards this so-called tool shed I think I am hallucinating.

"A shed . . . that? You must be joking?"

A mirage more like. A little circular building made of stone and carved wood, topped with a cracked dome. A ruin, standing beautiful and incongruous in the middle of a field. For a moment I struggle to find the right word to describe it, but I can't get it in French or in Italian.

"But . . . it looks like . . . a . . ."

"A chapel, yes. It is a chapel. Was sir not told?"

Mangini is clearly toying with me like a little school-boy. He points his finger at me and says: "You're the owner of a sacred place, *signor*!"

And he laughs all the louder.

I walk over towards it like a zombie with my hand stretched out in front of me. All the door needs is a gentle push and it crashes to the ground in a heap of dust.

"You really should be careful, *signor*!"

The dust makes me cough. I clamber over tools, harvesting baskets and secateurs lying on the chipped marble floor. A faded, crumbling mosaic of pink and black. When I look up I catch my breath in surprise seeing him there. Standing on a stone plinth with his hands in the air. The wood of his face flaking, his cheeks hollow and porous. But the eyes are harsh. Intact. Searching. His white tunic is disintegrating to dust. The cape must have been blue about a century ago. A junk shop saint. Only the look in his eye has stood the test of time. Still managing to be frightening. As if to deflate it, to annihilate it, someone has hung a succession of hooks and billhooks along the length of one arm. But it hasn't succeeded in making him look ridiculous. Whoever once sculpted that gaze must have lived in real fear and awe of all things sacred.

"Nothing damaged, Signor Polsinelli?" Mangini cries from outside.

I come back out, a little bewildered.

"Can you explain what this chapel's doing here?"

He laughs.

"We'll see about that tomorrow, no one's bothered about him for more than a hundred years, old Sant'Angelo, our protector. He can wait another night, can't he? Enjoy your walk . . ."

He heads straight off towards the hillside in the dwindling light. "And welcome, welcome, Signor Polsinelli . . ."

Soon all I can see of him is the gleam of his rifle butt through the leaves, and then I'm alone once more in this corner of the back of beyond, not knowing what I want or how I fit in. And, wherever I am, I'm the sort of person who starts feeling homesick as soon as night starts closing in. It doesn't take much. When I think of all the rootless people around the world.

... A country which would have made a deserter of me if I'd known it existed ... They needed ten volunteers per district, and they chose me to go to Albania. I'd never heard of it. I still couldn't tell you where it is to this day. Somewhere between Yugoslavia and Greece. Actually, we'd heard that they were going to launch the invasion of Greece from there. In fact one of our boys who was a bit more clued up said that Mussolini had thrown a tantrum, he wanted Greece but Hitler wouldn't agree to it, and the Duce wouldn't let it drop. A real tantrum ... Yup ... we were there because of his tantrums. That was all. I wanted to tell them that there were other guys who'd be better than me at playing invasions. That's all the fascists wanted to do. And none of us lot, Victor Emmanuel III's soldiers, none of us were invaders. We were all the same, trying to make ourselves small when the call-up came, slinking along the walls and making out the rifles were too heavy. Italians aren't really cut out for war, you know ... When an Italian garrison hears the order "Fix bayonets!" they think it's something about fixing hairnets and they head back to barracks. Everyone knows that. We had other things to think about instead of listening to lessons about courage. Mind you it took us twenty-eight days in a boat, the compare and me, to get to Tirana.

* * *

The landlady's TV was crackling with machine-gun fire, sirens and growling exhausts. With her eyes locked onto some bit of Americana, the young woman did manage to gesture towards the bowl of fritters in case I felt hungry. Just one was enough to line my stomach with lead for the rest of the evening, and, as if she could guess what I wanted, she took a bottle of red wine from a cupboard without taking her eyes off the big black cop reading his rights to the young hooligan he'd just arrested. For a moment I wondered what she actually got out of this exotic material. I sat down next to her on the sofa, with the bottle where I could reach it. We drank together without a word – her watching the end of her serial in reverential silence. Me quietly contemplating her profile.

"Are there blacks and Chinese in France too?"

"Yes."

"And the police doing stuff, at night, with car chases and noise, and girls?"

"Umm . . . Paris isn't New York, you know."

"There must be more going on than here, come off it . . . Nothing ever happens here."

"You can't say that. I haven't been here twenty-four hours and I've already seen all sorts of strange things."

She smiles but she doesn't believe me, and she hands her glass over for me to fill it up. She takes a sip and concentrates on the screen again. Perhaps because she's embarrassed. The tan on her shoulders and neck stops at the edge of her cheap smock dress, which is bunched up over her thighs. Underneath it I can make out a vest with one strap threatening to fall down. She slowly picks up the corners of the apron tied at her waist to fan her face. The police inspector says something that makes her laugh, but I didn't hear it. She raises her left leg to rest it on the arm of the sofa, making a slapping noise with her espadrille against her foot. Completely at ease. Is this the same girl who greeted me this morning? If it is, she's adopted me more quickly than I would have anticipated. I've got hundreds of questions I want to ask her, and she must have more than a thousand.

"Do you live here on your own?"

She has her answer ready. I even feel I've waited a bit too long before asking.

"Yes. My parents have left. I kept the *pensione* but I do other things for a living. Sewing, a lot of it. But also cooking and cleaning for older people in town."

She must be dying of boredom more than anything else, on her own all year long. In spite of her twenty-seven channels. When the serial comes to an end, she zaps. RAI have got some sort of show with very scantily clad girls. I feel a bit embarrassed. She turns the sound down, and I make the most of it.

"Is this local wine we're drinking?"

"Hmmph ... I make salad dressing with the local wine. The one you're drinking is from Barolo, my father used to love it, he left me quite a few bottles. Oh, if Sant'Angelo could see what was being made from his vineyard, he wouldn't protect us any longer!" she exclaims with a peal of shrill laughter.

I look at the label on the bottle. A 1974 Barolo.

"Could you tell the story of Sant'Angelo?"

Still looking at the twirling girls in sequins, she pours herself another glass and brandishes it high in the air.

"Blessings on our patron saint! Sant'Angelo visited us centuries ago, he appeared to some shepherds and he said 'It is here, on this land, that you will draw the blood of Christ!' That's what he said! I've never seen such long legs, look at that girl! *Ammazza* ... !"

I feel like telling her that she has legs too. But she probably doesn't realize it. For a moment I picture her without her tired clothes and I dress her up, and do her hair and make-up like a proper little Parisienne. A right bombshell who would turn every head on the Rive Droite.

"Do you know the little chapel in the middle of the vineyard over by Sant'Angelo?"

"Of course."

"What's it there for?"

"After the apparition they planted the vineyard and built the chapel, because it was the first time a saint had come all the way to our part of the world to visit us. They made the statue, and a priest used to come every Sunday and hold Mass for about thirty people. My grandmother was born not far from there, God rest her soul, and she knew it when it was open. Then one day they closed it down, there weren't enough people, it must have been about a hundred years ago. I stay in Sora when I go to church. I go with the old people."

"Don't you ever go to Rome?"

"Never. I watch the Easter Mass on TV. You can see the Pope right up close, and he does the Urbi et Orbi for us. He says it works even if you watch it on TV. My name's Bianca, by the way. Tell me, are you going to stay here long?"

"I don't know."

"Stay until the festival of Gonfalone at least, it's on the 12th of August. Everyone from the whole region'll be here, you'll see, all the villages gathered together, thousands of people!"

She glances quickly over to the big clock in the sitting room, gets up and changes channels.

"We nearly missed *Dallas*."

The music drools into our ears. She's already forgotten about me.

I was woken by the noise out in the street. I opened my blind to see the market teeming with life in every direction on the main square. The wine from the night before hadn't given me a headache. At the far end I could see Miss Quadrini buying a watermelon that was too heavy for her on top of her bag full of vegetables. She passed very close to the mad blind man sitting between two stalls playing his banjo. A passer-by throws him a coin, and he thanks her in song. Despite the distance I can hear him squealing and mimicking people. One of the market gardeners throws an apple at him to shut him up, and it hits the blind man right on the head. He freezes for a moment. He feels around, picks up the apple, gobbles it down and then yells:

"Hey, you cretin, next time, try a watermelon!"

Everyone laughs.

Convinced that I was alone in the house, I went to the kitchen to try and dig out some coffee, and recoiled slightly when I saw this guy sitting there with his arms crossed on the table and with a bag in front of him. About thirty, well dressed, fresh-faced, good teeth. A new customer? I don't know why but something in the way he looked at me made me think he was another nuisance – there was quite a conspiracy of them.

"Do you need a room?" I asked.

"No, I've come to see you, Mr Polsinelli."

Now, that nearly got me angry. I'm not making any effort to stay anonymous but I've got an unpleasant feeling there's a cross on my forehead.

"Let me introduce myself, Attilio Porteglia, I live in Frosinone, and I'd like to negotiate with you. I could try to talk in French, but which one of us knows the other's language best?"

"How did you know I was here?"

"You know what little villages are like . . ."

I shrug my shoulders. It does seem to be true that

anyone with the least interest in the vineyard doesn't have any trouble finding me.

Speaking clearly, he gave me an outline of the two or three aspects of his life that would help me understand why he was here. He was from a good family, he had studied wine in Paris and now wanted to launch his career in the field.

"I wanted to make my own wine, I have the money. One of the big French wine houses has agreed to undertake this venture with me."

"A French one?"

"Château-Lafite," he replied, trying to pronounce it the French way.

"And so . . .?"

"I want to settle in the area, I've had a look around, and I stumbled across your vineyard about a month ago. It's in exactly the sort of position I want for my future wine, and the acreage too, not more than 10,000 bottles a year, you could get more out of it but I wouldn't want to. I've tasted it and at the moment you couldn't say . . ."

"I know."

This is at least the tenth person who's told me the wine's disgusting. And I'm the only one who hasn't tasted it.

"I can't make a grand cru of it. Not a Château-Lafite, granted, but a good little wine which can make a name for itself."

"I don't know anything about it. Can it really be done?"

"You'd have to go right back to square one, to sacrifice the next three harvests, build a new cellar, buy oak barrels, and some . . . but . . . umm . . . why would I want to tell you all this . . ."

He stood up and opened his bag.

"I want this vineyard."

Wads of 50,000 lira notes.

"I'll buy it at twice its value per square yard, I'll give you 50 million lira in front of a solicitor. Plus what you see on the table here. Ten million lira if you make up your mind today."

"Put that away now, the woman who runs this place will be home any minute and I don't want her getting worried."

A little surprised, he put the wads of notes away and offered me the bag by the handle.

"No one will offer you more."

"And what if I wanted to make some? Good wine, I mean."

"You're joking, Signor Polsinelli . . ."

"Yes, I'm joking."

The Quadrini girl came home and greeted the stranger. I thought she seemed apprehensive, slightly awkward. She offered us a slice of watermelon, then some coffee. Over by the sofa I could see the bottle of wine from the previous evening.

"Do you have any more of that wine from last night?"

Without a word she went to find me another bottle.

"Signor Porteglia and I are going to have a little glass of wine, if you don't mind, Miss Quadrini?"

She shook her head and took two glasses from the cupboard for us. The young man raised his hand.

"No thank you, not for me, it's too early."

I looked him right in the eye as I wielded the corkscrew.

"You will have a glass with me!" I said, as if it were an order.

He realized straight away that he could not wriggle out of this. I didn't take my hand off the label for a moment. I put the bottle down at my feet. Bianca watched us.

Porteglia grudgingly looked at the colour of the wine, then smelled it and swirled it in his glass. As he brought it to his lips his eyes met mine.

A mouthful which he savoured for a few seconds. Then another. I drank mine down in one.

"So, what do you think of it?" I asked.

Porteglia doesn't take his eyes off his glass. His silence becomes prolonged. "Not easy. It all depends on how it's been kept."

"Come on . . . have a go. This should be child's play for an expert like you."

"It's from the North, I'm sure of that . . ."

"But I need more, Mr Porteglia. Be precise."

I found it quite amusing watching him sniffing at his glass, playing for time.

"I would say . . . umm . . . it's not a very eloquent wine . . . more austere, quite fruity. It lends itself well to ageing."

Fired up by the game, I poured myself another glass. Keeping the bottle well hidden under the table.

"This has coped quite well, but I don't think it should be kept for more than ten years."

After another sip he said: "I would guess it's from Piedmont."

"Stop beating about the bush, Mr Wine Expert. Say something."

"I would say it's a Barolo. Of an average vintage, but which has been kept for well over ten years."

I stopped drinking.

"Say . . . '74?"

Bianca let out a shrill little whistle. I thumped my glass down onto the table. Porteglia left without taking his bag, and said he would be back in the evening.

The Quadrini girl shows me the way to the post office. There's something equatorial about the place, a fan on the ceiling, little telephone kiosks in light wood, the counter in pink marble. The man behind it has a napkin tied round his neck and is putting away a plate- ful of pasta and sauce. With a twitch of his greasy jowls he makes it clear that I'm disturbing him. On the other end of the line, my mother asks whether it is hot, if I've found somewhere to eat and sleep. Apparently my father's promised that, as soon as he's back from his cure, he'll kick my arse for abandoning my mamma. He can talk!

In the afternoon I went back to the vineyard where Signor Mangini was waiting for me with the man who worked the vines (who'd put on his Sunday best). An impressionable young man, this Giacomo. Not only was I probably the first foreigner, apart from Dario, he'd ever spoken to in his life, but – more importantly – I was *il padrone*. First and foremost he wanted to unleash on me a great wave of technical patter about his work methods, the type of vine, the wine-making process, pruning the vines, and a whole stack of things I didn't know about but I tried to look interested. The vineyard wasn't his real job, but his own farm wasn't going well, and for a few years he'd been trying to make a bit of money from these vines that no one could be bothered to tend. He managed to sell a few thousand bottles to a chain of staff canteens in Milan, but he was much more enthusiastic about Dario's offer of a salary. If Dario trusted this poor man to make his wine, then that's further proof that he couldn't give a damn about the quality of the stuff. They took me into the cellars that had been dug out under the barn. I saw a long line of barrels holding the 30,000 litres of unsold wine that had accumulated over the last four years. I at last succeeded in moistening my lips with the stuff for the first time. I'd heard so much about it that I nearly winced as I came into contact with it. They waited, anxiously, for my first reaction.

"Well?"

Well, I just pretended. With a profoundly meditative expression, I gargled it backwards and forwards over my palate, waiting for something to happen. It didn't feel like drinking the blood of Christ. Yesterday's Barolo was a cruel point of comparison. But I was expecting much worse. It is pretty pungent, it's true. The sort of thing you'd get in a carafe, rather like the cheap quarter bottle in a café, probably accompanying a croque monsieur and washed down with a cup of coffee, otherwise it would give you a crashing headache for the rest of the afternoon. I didn't spit it out; that would have made the poor boy who toiled to produce the stuff lower his eyes in shame.

"Well???"

Well, I put a bit more into the ladle, saddling myself with another mouthful. This time I drank it straight down, as if I were thirsty, and the other two didn't follow my lead. I would have liked to have found something to say, something original, too this or not enough that. In fact there wasn't anything to say. It was wine. And one that was not pretentious enough to get by without a good plateful of food. I once heard a chef saying that Italian cooking was the second in the world, because it was the second in the world to understand wine as food.

What could Dario have been thinking, dragging his patent leather shoes into this backwater?

"Well, what does sir think, hey?"

* * *

Three days of traipsing about and sniffing round the land, the town, in people's houses, hoping for a spark of intuition. The solicitor who wished me good luck after reading through every last paragraph of the title deeds. And the assistant mayor too, anyone who was anyone in Sora, but they couldn't give me a clue. Two new attempts by Porteglia, during which I took great pleasure in doubling the sum. With that I could go back to Paris and take two years' holiday. But Dario had been planning to retire at 30 thanks to this piece of land. Giacomo's working hard towards the next harvest; he and his two workmen are cutting the leaves that cast their shadows over the grapes, and sparing those that protect them from the rain. But it won't rain this year. It'll be a good harvest. I walked up and down the land for hours at a time, not missing a single square inch. I even scratched at the earth in a few places, chosen at random, to reveal some treasure. Vain hope. But I had to get it out of my system. The longer this goes on the more I feel that there isn't anything to find. There's just work here, nothing but work, and Dario always ran away from work. Yesterday evening when I was completely exhausted I went to complain to the true *padrone* of this land: Sant'Angelo himself. And what if the treasure wasn't buried but well and truly out in the open where everyone could see it for the last century, like the statue or the chapel? Wasted effort, the chapel was going to fall apart any minute and the plinth for the statue was hollow but empty. As for Sant'Angelo himself, a child could have taken him and flogged him in the market without anyone noticing. But I did spot something strange in the chapel, cracks in various places that looked as if they'd been made deliberately. And others that looked as if they'd been patched up with brackets and beams nailed to the roof structure. The locals think I'm mad. I miss my father more and more. Sometimes I feel as if I'm at the front, in a foreign country, without ever actually seeing the enemy.

. . . We landed at the port of Durrës to travel to Tirana, the capital. We saw fascists there, and we were used to that but I was really scared when we saw Germans too, real Germans, until someone told us that those boys were our allies. Our allies? Them? And a whole lot more rubbish like that, like trying to tell us Albania had been annexed to us since '39. So what? What the hell was that to us? They posted us to what they called an air base and we stayed there for four months doing nothing except watch the sky through binoculars, and at night we tried to detect them by ear while we played cards. If and when there was a suspect noise, we'd ring through to the anti-aircraft gun, but we never actually heard the thing fire. And that's it. An enemy? No, no enemy. No one. My compare *and I began to think we weren't really needed there. One day we were told there was something that needed defending. What was it? An oil well. Yes . . . Ten soldiers standing round an oil well for a year and a half. And no one wanted to attack it. That was in '43, and we were told that terrible things were happening in Europe, we feared for our loved ones while we were sleeping round an oil well for more than eighteen months. The war was going on less than three hundred miles from our oil well . . . three hundred . . . At one point I was given a fortnight's leave. My* compare *said, "Don't take it, you'll run more risks going home than staying here." And he was right. Fifteen days in Sora and four whole months to make the return journey. I thought they'd label me a deserter in Albania. My arse . . . No one even noticed . . . And like an idiot I went back to all those sleepyheads when I could have stayed at home, and really deserted. But the* compare *was waiting for me with tears in his eyes. When I asked if he'd seen*

any enemies in those months, he said no, and I went off to bed.

Bianca waited for me before having supper. Without saying so, of course.

"Penne all'arrabbiata?"

Yes! I said, famished. Penne is like short macaroni, cut diagonally. And the sauce is "rabid" because it's made at great speed and it's spicy.

"When my mother makes a sauce it takes a good three hours," I say.

"It should. A real tomato sauce takes either less than ten minutes or more than two hours, because in between you get all the acidity of the tomatoes. Tomorrow I'll make cannelloni, if you like, Antonio. . ."

She blushes a little for saying that and I can't think where to put myself. On the table there's a huge bowl of pistachios. I taste a couple of them.

"Would you switch the TV on please, Antonio?"

She can't live without it. I'm afraid that everything she knows about the world is contained in that box of pictures.

"There's nothing good on at the moment, but it helps me with the cooking."

"Sorry?"

"Of course it does . . . Here, I'll teach you how to make arrabbiata sauce. It's quarter to eight. Put RAI on."

A jingle introducing a sequence of advertisements.

"Put the water on to boil and at the same time heat a whole clove of garlic in a really hot pan until the end of the ads."

The smell of the simmering garlic wafts over to me. The ads come to an end. She asks me to zap onto the fifth channel where a boy standing in front of a map of Italy is predicting 95°F tomorrow.

"As soon as he starts the weather you can take the garlic out of the oil. You don't need it any more, all the taste has gone into the oil. Put the peeled tomatoes into the pan. When he's finished the weather the water'll be boiling, tip the penne in. Switch to Channel Four."

A gameshow presenter, an audience, hostesses, giant dice, numbers lighting up, excited participants.

"When they give the results of the draw, you can stir the sauce a bit, and add a little tin of tomato purée, just to give it a bit of colour, a couple of little chillies, no more, and leave it on a high heat, don't cover it, it'll spit all over the place but they say that an arrabbiata sauce is only really good when the kitchen's splattered with red. Switch to channel two."

A Brazilian soap opera filmed on video, two rather starchy lovers arguing in a living room.

"At the end of the episode it's the news and it'll be time to eat. The sauce and the pasta will be ready at exactly the same time. Fifteen minutes. Did you get that?"

Without realizing it I had accumulated a little pile of pistachio shells in front of me. Nervously, I eat a couple more. The worst thing for dulling your appetite.

"Beware the curse of the pistachios, Antonio! They say that when Christ was fleeing the Pharisees he took refuge in a field of pistachio trees. But when you shake one of the branches, it makes a chiming noise, and the Pharisees found him straight away. So he said, 'Whosoever shall eat a single one of these seeds will never be able to sate himself.' You should eat olives instead.'"

She is more and more adorable, with her cooking, her recipes and her fables and legends.

"Olives are the same," I said.

"No, no they're not. Christ took refuge in an olive grove once, but because the trunk of an olive tree is hollow no one found him and he blessed the olive tree."

If all this is true, I'll ask her to be my wife, and if it isn't, I'll marry her. Mind you, I didn't know that Christ was such a coward.

"Your recipe's not bad but I don't have a TV."

"Well, you'll have to eat chickpeas."

The steaming hot pasta arrived on my plate. A delicacy to set the palate on fire. I've always been wary of girls who know how to cook.

"How old are you, Bianca?"

"I was born in '61."

"I don't believe you. Which month?"

"September."

". . . Really? Which day?"

"The first. I'm very proud of it. And if you want to be even more precise, it was three o'clock in the afternoon."

Incredible . . . I'm just four short hours older than her. Hardly enough time to get used to the sounds of this world. I'm so disturbed by this coincidence that I look at my hostess rather differently now. The first of September?

Even though our lives are so different they have overlapped in many ways. With her here and me over there, all the experiences of childhood, the milestones, the hopes, right up to the moment where the adult emerged. As if we'd lived everything in reverse to end up together that evening. If I'd been born here, a couple of streets from her home, we'd probably have come across each other thousands of times without ever really talking.

A delicious silence, maintained by bouts of shy eye contact, settled between us. I swore to myself that I would take her in my arms before going back to France. But I didn't quite have the courage that night. I soon abandoned her and the empty plates. Her eyes full of loneliness.

A prowler. Me. At night. I'm more comfortable in this role than that of the boss. This evening I have every intention of properly confronting the angel with the stony eyes. He might be able to tell me what it is about this place.

> *The sky is black in the day and in the night again*
> *How sad, how sad to see only in black . . .*

This time the blind man didn't succeed in catching me unawares. I knew he'd come back. His singing gave him away. They say the blind have a good ear. Perhaps, but only when they're sober. When they're drunk they're just like anyone else, thuggish, noisy and alone in the world. I move towards the barrel next to which he's taken up residence for the night. Falstaff with the blank stare of the dead.

Splayed on the ground, his belly full to bursting, he froze for a moment when he sensed there was someone there. I actually got to see his eyes. They wandered and I thought that he would have to fumble on the ground for a long time to find his glasses, but they were back on his nose in no time. I went right up to him in absolute silence. He just got on and took another slug of wine. The spinning in his head would give him trouble identifying a whole battalion of circus artists.

I went as close as I could, to spy on him, to stand over him, like a warrior watching a wounded man crawling

91

at his feet on the battlefield. He emptied a bottle and sang again.

> *One day a man came,*
> *He promised me gold*
> *But he died before he was old*

Then he chucked the bottle up in the air, and it nearly hit me full in the face. If I hadn't ducked it I'd be short of an eye as I speak. You could say it would have taught me not to snoop on people.

"Who was this man?" I shouted, to make him jump.

He moved like a worm that you haven't succeeded in squashing, writhing and wrapping himself round a tree. After a few moments of pure fear and drunken grumbling, he begged me not to hurt him.

"I know who you are! The Frenchman! You speak like the Frenchman!"

"Who was this man who promised you gold?"

"I won't drink your wine any more, I swear, please don't hit me!"

I picked up the ladle that was lying on the floor, filled it with wine and went over towards him gently.

"You can drink all the wine that's here, I don't give a damn. And that's from the boss himself, go on, drink, have it . . ."

He's so used to being thrashed the minute he sets foot in the place that he doesn't believe me. "Drink!" I said, as if giving him an order.

He did so straight away, I don't think he interpreted it as a welcoming gesture, and he was right. I just thought that the more drunk he got the more chance I'd have of getting him to spit out some clue, some inkling about whatever it was that was fishy in this little kingdom of mine.

"Who was he, this rich man?"

"What are you trying to find on this land? What is it that you French want, this isn't your country . . ."

He carried on drinking without further encouragement. When he said "you French" I sensed that I was on the right tracks. His song had intrigued me when I very first heard it. The story of his life in a nutshell. A worn-out old litany like a nagging remorse. I asked him again about the man and the promise of gold.

"Was he a Frenchman like me?"

As soon as he nodded my heart started racing.

"He was my friend, you know . . . Did he promise you money?"

"Too much money . . . And other things too, better things . . . Don't make me think about it, please, give me some wine, he was the chance of a lifetime for me. . ."

"What did he want? Tell me!"

"I want some wine . . ."

He started to cry and I suddenly felt that he was close to admitting everything, although, unfortunately, I was equally sure that he wouldn't utter another word the whole night, despite the alcohol, and despite the tears. And there was absolutely no question of letting that happen. Furious, I clenched my fists. I remembered that he was frightened of being hit. Another wave of anger rose up in me and every nerve in my body wanted to lash out at him again but this time, by some extraordinary reflex, he managed to duck at the right moment. And my hand rammed straight into the tree.

At the first glimmer of light the drunk fell asleep.

I'll remember that day for the rest of my life.

That day I watched a man go to the very extremity of drunkenness, a creature wrapped in fire, ablaze with the longing to spit it all out at last, everything about himself and the world, feeding the flames with great quaffs of alcohol. That day I heard a voice making revelations that broke the last barriers of secrecy, its very apotheosis. You can't witness something like that just by listening half-heartedly. No one could have resisted it, not even a priest. And in this particular case, especially not a priest. I couldn't cope any longer, I started drinking too, so that I could take it all in and hold out to the very end.

Then he collapsed heavily in my arms. I didn't know that a human being could have so much strength when it came to telling their life story. I got up and headed back to the *pensione* to forget it all. My head was spinning from so many words and from the bad wine. I thought I might sink and go under in that damp soil, and no one would ever know. I clenched my fists to stop myself being sick, shapeless images kept crashing in on my mind, everything became confused, my life and his, as if I had to cling to his memories so as not to go under.

. . . In November '43 everything changed. They gathered us together at the foot of a hill to give us some important news. There were 70,000 soldiers in all, each of us anxious at the

thought of meeting there like that, all together. There were fascists and Germans there too. That was when one of the officers started to speak from the top of the hill. He said: "The armistice has been signed with the Greeks!" We pretty much took that as good news until he added, "Run for your lives!" At first we didn't really understand what he meant, but when we saw submachine guns appearing from behind the hill we began to wonder. When they started firing at us, we thought explanations could wait till later. Two years in that country without a single enemy or a single battle, and it had to be Italians who shot us like rabbits. Mind you, the worst thing about it all – and you'll never believe this . . . it's sad to say, but we felt like orphans. I can't think of another word for it. The Italian state had just withdrawn from the whole business and left us there. It was like a father leaving home and abandoning his children. Exactly like that. Exactly . . . We were free, demobilized, and from that moment on it was even worse than before. We tried to get to the ports but we knew there wouldn't be any boats waiting to take us home. The fascists and the Germans were carrying on fighting, I don't know to this day who with, but we were allowed to go home. But we couldn't. We met Albanian partisans for the first time. We tried to speak their language. We almost made friends. I gave them my rifle, because they knew what to do with it, they said. And that was a good move because if I'd hesitated I might not be here now to tell the tale. We were no longer in uniform. It was winter.

Tripping and stumbling, I got back to the path, and I walked as best I could, like the blind man but without his ability or his treachery. I teetered from tree to tree for a long time, convinced that I'd covered most of the route when I'd actually gone less than three hundred feet. For a moment I thought I'd never manage it and that, despite my best efforts, I'd fall into a ditch and have to wait for someone to get me out.

I didn't have to wait long.

Despite the fact that my eyes were half-closed and hazy, I could just make out the silent little car turning off and sidling up to me incredibly slowly. It knocked into my legs, and I fell onto the bonnet and tried to hang on there. I didn't feel any impact. The car stopped and I didn't have the strength to get back to my feet. Somewhere in the spinning inside my skull I did, however, grasp the fact that the aim of their game was not actually to run me over.

A silhouette appeared. I was sick all over the windscreen.

"It would have been so easy to knock you down and continue quietly on my way."

The voice didn't mean anything to me. I had to screw my eyes right up to try to recognize it. I was foggily aware that I was entering the critical phase of inebriation, that ill-defined zone which marks the transition between euphoria and nausea, that brief moment when you would give the world just to collapse in a heap and be left in peace. The bastard had got to me at that precise moment.

"But it's not you I want, it's your land."

At the same time the strange chemistry that occurs between the alcoholic vapours and the complexities of the mind mean that, in spite of everything, you feel lucid, probably far too lucid. And you don't give a damn about anything, about anything that could happen. When I heard the word "land" I burst out laughing. Just as I had puked up the wine, I now spewed a great stream of words, but in my own language this time, and I can't tell you how good it felt speaking French. Whingeing in French, hurling insults in French, laughing at someone in French.

"You can do better than that, Signor Polsinelli. I made you a serious – and generous – offer. But if you continue to refuse, you'll never see the last of me."

Porteglia. I recognized him at last. I thought to myself that his mask had fallen away a bit more quickly than expected.

"Fuck off . . ."

"If I were you, *signor* . . ."

"Fuck off, I'm drunk and you can bugger off . . ."

He disappeared for a moment, only to reappear with something long, thin and shiny in his hand.

"Of your own free will or under duress you will eventually hand over this vineyard. But there isn't much time, I need it quickly. You'll only die sooner if you don't sell it to me. I'll follow you all the way to France to bleed you dry."

He brought the thing up to my face and drew a line with it up my cheek. A sharp, rather hot feeling. When he'd taken it out from under my eyebrow I could see what it was. An open razor, pure and simple. Like the one the barber had used in Rome. It was probably the first time I'd seen one so close up. When the stream of blood reached my neck, I remembered how I'd crawled on the floor at home after the gunshot, the smell of the pure alcohol, and all those partygoers on the terrace opposite.

"Do you still refuse to discuss it?"

I waited a moment before replying.

"Even more so . . . after . . . last night . . ."

Because since that night I'd started to understand what was being cooked up on this piece of land. I finally grasped that it wasn't enough just tending the soil, turning it over and digging it up to get something out of it. First and foremost, you had to own it. That's why this bastard wasn't actually going to kill me now.

On the other hand, he did know that I could no longer go to the police.

"I hope you understand this, Signor Polsinelli, just having your name on a piece of paper isn't really all it takes to own this land. The locals will never forgive you, look what happened to your friend Dario. And you'll end like him, for the same reasons . . ."

"*Va fan'cullo . . .*"

His blade came to rest against my neck.

I waited for him to slice.

A split second.

Then I heard a loud bang.

Porteglia collapsed against me. My head smacked back into the windscreen and we both fell down onto the road. I clenched my teeth to stop myself passing out. Head against head. His trickling against mine. My cheek couldn't pull away from his forehead. I lost consciousness.

* * *

A vaulted ceiling, filthy, full of cracks. Grass growing up between the flagstones. And a saint with his hands in the air, watching me from up there.

Paradise . . .

Still only half conscious, I dragged myself over to the statue to check that the two of us were still part of the material world. I cried out, stroking the stone plinth.

I felt safe in the chapel, and Sant'Angelo must have watched over me. He kept me alive. I automatically brought my hands up to my face and then my neck. Nothing. Not a snick.

"What the hell am I doing here, *benedetto* Sant' Angelo? What is it? Have I got to speak in Italian before you'll deign to reply . . . have I? But I'm fed up with speaking Italian."

Outside the blind man had disappeared. Further away along the track I looked for Porteglia's car, afraid that I'd find his body lying nearby, but all I found were a few smears of blood where we'd fallen. His, mine, who would ever know?

So as not to frighten Bianca, I kept my head turned as I went through the kitchen. Pointless precaution: she hadn't come back from the market yet, I saw her from the window negotiating the daily watermelon. There was a note for me on the table: "There's food in the fridge and the bed is made up." I packed my bag in a few moments and rushed back to the kitchen to scribble my own note on the piece of paper. "I'm going away for a few days, but will be back for the Gonfalone." And I went out.

Four hours later I was in the coach heading for the capital. As on the outward journey, I sat right next to the driver. Amongst other things, my time in Rome would help erase the spectre of the night I had just lived through, it would mean I could get a few days' sleep before taking this momentous step, and – most importantly – it would give me a chance to prove on paper that Dario was as brilliant as he'd made out. I must get back to the village for the Gonfalone. Everything converges on that date, the 12th of August. After that I'll know whether all this has been worth the trouble. And I'll go back home with a happy heart, knowing that at least I've tried to prolong the dream of a childhood friend.

As we passed it, I glanced over at the Coliseum and then at the monument of Victor Emmanuel. The Romans call the first "The Camembert"and the second

"The Typewriter". Even if they do both look like their nicknames, I'm not sure many Romans have actually seen a camembert up close. I instinctively got out near the station to look for a room, and it didn't take long. All I had to do was go into the first restaurant I came across and one of the waiters gave me the address of the best *pensione* with the best beds and the best hot water in the whole area, and – as if I hadn't already cottoned on – he told me that I should mention his name. He also dropped into the conversation the fact that he served the best tagliatelle in the whole street.

A few hours later I woke up in a *matrimoniale* bed where there was enough room for a newly married couple and several witnesses. It had cost 10,000 lira extra but I didn't regret it. The manager was a tall, bearded man of about fifty who was quite friendly and not against a bit of a chat with the customers if it was about his beloved city. While he was making the lunch.

"How long will you be staying with us?"

"I have to be back on the morning of the 11th."

He took a strand of spaghetti out of the boiling water, examined it without actually tasting it, threw it back into the water and turned off the gas.

"Just three days . . .? Do you know how many it took to build Rome?"

"It wasn't built in one, everyone knows that. So how come it took only one night to burn it?"

"Come on . . . that's just tittle tattle!" he said, shaking the colander.

"Don't you taste it before serving it?"

"I never do, but everyone has their own way of doing it. I look at it, and that's enough. But I can prove that it's just right much more surely than you can by tasting it."

He picked up a piece of spaghetti and threw it against the wall.

"There, look. If it was still raw it wouldn't stick, and if it was overdone it would slip down. We can cook it to perfection here because we're at sea level."

"What do you mean?"

"Didn't you know that you can't cook pasta the same by the sea and up in the mountains? At higher altitudes water has a lower boiling point, it doesn't boil hard enough, so it's impossible to cook really fine pasta because it has to be done very quickly when the water's really boiling otherwise it just turns to glue. That explains a lot about regional specialities. Oh . . . you've landed on your feet here! I know it all, the lot, everything! You absolutely have to see the ceiling of Saint Cecilia's, right by the Pantheon, and while you're in the area, you ought to . . ."

"I don't think I'll have time."

"What did you come here for then? The restaurants? The local girls?"

"The libraries."

"*Prego* . . . ?"

"I need to do some research in libraries. Do you know any?"

He hesitated for a moment then turned towards the corridor and called loudly:

"Alfredo . . .! Alfredo . . .! *Ma dove sei, ammazza . . .!* Alfredo . . .!"

"A young boy of about fifteen appeared in the corridor."

"It's for you," said the father. "An intellectual . . ."

The tourist information office wouldn't have done any better. Young Alfredo understood what I needed straight away and recommended the two places where

101

I would find what my heart desired, as well as the address of the French bookshop, La Procure, in case my Italian suddenly let me down.

For two whole days I consulted, trawled through and photocopied the documents I needed, and as each hour went by I watched the project develop with the distinct impression that everything had been set up and ready for a long time. In fact, all I had to do was walk in the footsteps that Dario had so kindly left. In the evening I shut myself away with my file and the surveyor's plans of the land to see whether all this madness had any chance of holding together. During the night, after spending a long time calculating various parameters, I made endless rather scruffy and clumsy sketches before eventually ending up with something that seemed clear. Luminous. And when I looked at this strange combination, all the cogs in this improbable mechanism, I wondered whether I would one day have any right to eternal rest. After all, it might be because of this that Dario was punished; the chastisement had come from a higher power, you might say. How could a plan like this have been formed in such a tiny head? It's enough to make you think that lazy bastards can be geniuses when it comes to making others do the work . . . and not just people.

I've never missed you as much as I do now, Dario . . . I'm frightened and it's your fault. I might be heading for disaster by trying to help your plan outlive you. It can't work, this idea of yours. It's unthinkable . . . it's mad, do you know what I mean? You were the best at your little local con tricks and your two-bit dodgy deals but this is too big for you. For us. Thanks for the present. And I don't mean the vineyard but the Pandora's box that goes with it, and that I'm going to be stupid enough to open soon. I'm sure you're right there looking at us, and you're laughing as you watch all these little people getting worked up. You'll have a front row seat tomorrow. You'll get your vendetta, and then I'll come and give you a piece of my mind on the spot if this all turns sour.

"Couldn't you stay a little longer, just two or three days? You can't leave without seeing San Paolo fuori le Mura, San Pietro in Vincoli with the statue of Moses by Michelangelo, and . . ."

Alfredo's dad is really putting his heart into it; it's sacrilegious to be leaving so soon, but I've promised to come back.

"Really, I can't, and the only saint I'm interested in is one no one else much cares about."

"Which one's that?"

"Sant'Angelo."

Now there, there was a long silence . . .

"He's no longer listed in the Vatican's directory, I've looked."

"Are you sure he's one of ours?"

"Oh definitely . . . he's the most Italian of all the saints. The most Italian in the world."

A little surprised, he shrugged his shoulders.

"And why's that . . .?"

I knew what to say, but I felt happier keeping my mouth shut.

*   *   *

Friday 11th August, 4.30 p.m.

Just another half hour in the coach and I'll be back in the little village. During the journey I've worked on my rough sketches, scribbling over them again and again. I want to see Bianca again. When I tried to go to

103

sleep I couldn't get away from various images which, like so much else that was happening to me, were not controlled entirely by me.

 . . . . *From that November until January '44 five of us found ourselves alone out in the snow. We built a shelter in the mountains, I found a knife so we could make baskets and we used them to barter with the Albanian farmers for a handful of corn and some beans, and the* compare *– who didn't know how to do anything except cook – would serve them up for us in the evenings. Three spoonfuls each, and all of us taking sideways glances at the over-filled spoonfuls the others were taking. No salt, but when we did find any we'd put a pinch of it on our tongues before eating. We were dirty and shabby, I had a big knitted vest with a flea in every stitch. I was well aware that we weren't an invading force. Three months of trying to find information, listening to the rumours about the boats leaving for home. I ended up begging. One night I headed off towards a military hospital I'd heard people talking about. Nearly 60 miles. When I got there I was half dead with exhaustion and hunger. They told me I had two arms and two legs, and they requisitioned me to bury the dead bodies so that the dogs wouldn't eat them. I put one underground with his name and number in a bottle around his neck. I wasn't feeling that bad, after all, and I went back to the others. That was when the* compare *made me swear not to abandon him.*

Sora, the end of the line. They're hanging blue garlands on the main square where the procession will start tomorrow. To create a bit of atmosphere, the blind man is shouting "Higher! Higher!"and waving his stick in the air, and everyone's laughing. There are children who are already excited about the festivities running around brandishing little flags in the town's colours of blue and yellow. People from Rome have come specially for the Gonfalone and they get off the bus with me. I head straight for Bianca's house and find her talking to new customers from neighbouring regions. The *pensione*'s going to be full to bursting tonight. She breaks off mid sentence when she sees me.

"You're lucky. I could have let out your room ten times."

Children scampering about the kitchen, a baby's bottle warming, couples sitting themselves down.

"Thankfully there's only one Gonfalone a year, *ammazza* . . . These kids are going to break my TV."

When she mentioned her TV I was reminded of a programme I'd discovered while I was in Rome. A magazine programme you wouldn't get anywhere else but in Italy. If I can actually get through this carpet of kids clustered round watching a crappy cartoon, I might have a slim chance of catching it. Bianca has taken great pleasure in zapping onto RAI Uno to come to my help and, at the same time, to establish her omnipotence over the little flickering box.

Eleven o'clock in the evening. The town is quieter and the good people are saving their energies for tomorrow. Let them sleep in peace, they're going to have their eyes opened wide.

I make a note of how many minutes it takes to get to the vineyard, walking slowly. The blind man is waiting for me there, as agreed, in the place we last parted company. The old drunk knows the land better than anyone else ever will. He doesn't understand anything I tell him about the end of that other night. He's not surprised someone attacked me, but he swears on the head of Sant'Angelo that he had completely lost consciousness.

"Don't let them intimidate you, *padrone* . . . Tomorrow they won't be able to touch you."

Should I believe him? Tomorrow might be the beginning of another nightmare. In the meantime, I need to set things up, and the blind man is prepared to do whatever it takes to help me. We stay there a good hour going over the whole plan, repeating each stage and operation a thousand times, starting with the shortcut to the vineyard across the corn field and avoiding the path. Inside the chapel I shine the beam of my torch onto the saint's face, and take out the aerosol that I bought in Rome.

"Don't worry, now . . . it's for your own good."

I completely cover the crumbling wood with the transparent suspension. The smell is terrible but they did assure me that it would fade in a few hours. I look at the Protector's face again. Before leaving him I give him a pat on the cheek.

"The ball's in your court!" I tell him.

The blind man turns round.

"Who are you talking to? Him? Have you gone mad, *padrone* . . .?"

"I'm not the *padrone*. He is."

Before going out I cast one last admiring glance at the way Dario reworked the roof structure, with the real crack deftly carved out amongst the false ones, the areas that he replastered and those that he exposed, the beams held in place by flimsy pieces of wood. At first sight, it's even better thought out than the projects architects get me to work on. We'll soon see.

We go and drink a little glass of wine. In his case to celebrate God alone knows what, in mine to give me some Dutch courage. We use the time to sort out the last details of our absurd venture. He mentions two or three little things that hadn't occurred to me. Dario, on the other hand, had thought them through carefully. Simple little points but ones which bring the whole thing together, like the bucket of wine which needs to be filled straight away this evening to save time, and put next to the statue. I hope my late friend has thought of everything. He had to go and die for me to realize his talents.

"Us Italians have lots of faults, but we do have one saving grace," says the blind man. "We're copers. Shambolic, I'll grant you. Disorganized, yes. But we can improvise. Improvisation! Dario could do it, and so can you, Antonio."

I'm not sure that it's a compliment.

"I've got to get back to Sora. Where are you going to sleep?"

"Don't worry about me, *padrone*."

We sit in silence for a moment. When I think of him it's as "the blind man", and I don't even know his name.

"What's your name?"

"Marcello. But no one's ever asked me."

"What are you going to do . . . after . . .?"

"Oh, well . . . I'll live. And I'll buy myself a rainbow."

I took one last walk over the land before getting back onto the path. It's the path my father used to take to exercise his turkeys. Not far from my family farm which no longer exists.

. . . One day we'd had enough of going round in circles, the compare *and me, of buggering up our lives and having nothing to eat. So for more than a year we worked the land for any Albanians who would take us on. It's stupid to work the land in another country when your own is lying fallow. Corn, cabbages. Tobacco plantations too. What a joy that tobacco was. The only comfort we had. At night, when the bosses couldn't see, I would cook up the leaves but the problem was the paper. One day I found a book in Greek – I'd like to have known what it was about – and I cut it into strips to roll*

cigarettes. That book lasted me fifteen months. The only book I've held in my hand in my whole life and I smoked it. There was plenty of meat, hares, wild boar, but the Albanians didn't touch it – because of their religion, they said. We had to light fires at night to keep the boars off the crops. Keeping them away instead of eating them! One day I told a group of children that hare tasted good. Perhaps if they eat hare over there nowadays it might be partly thanks to me.

Bianca's pretending to watch the screen. In fact, she's waiting for me. I know that from her secret smile when I come into the room, from the simple fact that she's still there after such a hard day's work, but mostly I know it from what she's wearing, naive and rather touching. She's dressed somewhere between Sunday best and New Year's Eve, between black and white, between well-behaved and mischievous. With quite a lot of lipstick.

She takes two ice-creams from the freezer and puts them on a tray near the sofa. Melon and blackberry sorbet.

"Tell me about Paris . . ."

"Pfff . . . there's not much to say."

I say that so as not to rush her, when I'm actually thinking exactly the opposite.

The TV's so loud I find it difficult to think. I zap and settle for a black and white film, some sort of melodrama that's quite restful on the eyes and ears. Then I put the tray down on the floor and I take her in my arms for a melon and blackberry flavoured kiss. I move my lips down to cool her neck.

She didn't want me to undress her, and she slipped into bed first. I liked the half light which smudged out all the rustic aspects of the room, and I waited till her body had shaken off the flashy clothes which belonged

108

to another era. As I ran my hand over her nakedness draped in white, I left the town and even the whole country to travel somewhere quite different, in a dream that was simple and somehow familiar, like coming home, where everything is straightforward again. And yet, as our bodies pressed together and pounded into each other in the darkness, I could make out the looks, the beginnings of gestures, the unspoken sentences, the expectations briefly coinciding, the fleeting affairs and the pent-up desires. In her as well as in me.

A long time afterwards she laughed and said: "Even if you don't want to and even when you're silent, you're telling me about Paris, Antonio."

Comings and goings in the corridor, stifled giggles from scampering children and, to top it all, Bianca's quasi-military wake up call when she rapped on the door. This all contributed to making me open my eyes.

"I waited till the last minute to wake you. You're going to miss the beginning of the procession."

"Are you coming to the *fiera*, Bianca?"

"I've got to look after my old people, and some friends have left their baby with me. Apparently a local TV crew are going to film the games, so I won't miss everything."

Without rushing I have a shower and a cup of coffee, and I watch the main square out of the kitchen window. The whole village is already there, abuzz, men, women, children, and *tutti quanti*. Bianca's probably going to be the only person left to take care of Sora. There won't be anything to watch, though, the low-lifes and the thieves will all be at the *fiera*. My father often used to tell me about the Gonfalone. The five villages coming together, each bearing its own colours, like Indian tribes who meet up once a year and decide to assemble as a single nation. It takes the procession almost an hour to reach the crossroads between the five villages. Everything has been set up there, a huge ring where the men selected for the games will make superhuman efforts to see their flag triumph. Tug-of-war, arm wrestling and other demonstrations of muscular prowess. All around it there are stands, tables, a gigantic fair, a riot of fun and noise that lasts all day. And when the winning village has been chosen and fêted, everyone forgets everything, the colours, the villages, the flags and the games. All that's left are thousands of individuals, drunk on the events of the day and ready to go on late into the night.

The crowd is growing visibly and, megaphone in hand, the mayor greets everyone. I get dressed, now hurrying a little so as not to miss the moment when the procession moves off. I rush into the great gathering and look everywhere to see where Marcello might have put himself. I can hear his shaky singing very close by, he's scratching at his banjo and giving his rendition of a local popular song to the delight of those around him. I still find his dark glasses just as terrifying. But then, setting the scene properly is his job. The mayor gives the signal for the departure and I find myself wedged between two women laden with baskets. In front of me I can see Mangini talking to some people; he turns and waves to me. Marcello is led by the arm by a young man who sings along with him in a canon.

I'm frightened.

There's still time to put an end to this farce.

Without even realizing it, I'm dragging my feet. The cordon of people behind me are pushing me gently, as if to convince me that it's too late and that I should have done my thinking before. It's only now that I'm calculating the risks. There are too many of them. Something in Dario's plan could go wrong, and then I won't be risking prison but eternal damnation.

We turn into the road that passes close to the path out to the vineyard. We're walking too quickly, I got my timings wrong. My heart starts beating faster, I clench my teeth. I look for Marcello everywhere, but can't see him. The young man who was guiding him is now

111

chatting to a girl. The blind man has slipped away, as planned. I look at my watch, ten minutes and we'll be passing close by the godforsaken piece of land. Now's the time to talk to the locals, now or never. I pass quite close to Mangini who waves again, and we fall into conversation but I can't even understand a word he's saying any more, it's the fear, I can't hear anything, he's smiling. What the hell's the blind man doing? I look at my watch three times in quick succession, people laugh, everything is becoming more and more of a blur, I'm frightened.

"Are you going to stay in our country long?"

Marcello, what the hell are you doing? Dario, damn you, this is all your fault. The blue and yellow banner is just about to pass the little path.

"Signor Polsinelli . . .? Can you hear me . . .?"

"What?"

"I was asking whether you were going to stay in Italy for long . . ."

I can't speak.

And what if I went home right now? Backtracked, without taking my bag, without saying goodbye to anyone, walked to the nearest station, waited for the train to Rome, got back to Paris . . .

"You'll have to come and have supper with me before you go, won't you? Signor Polsinelli . . .? Are you feeling all right?"

My heart's going to explode, my head's going to explode, I can see the first vines, in two minutes' time the procession will have gone past the path and the whole thing will be cocked up. Marcello, Dario, and you too, you the Patron Saint, you've abandoned me . . .

"You need to lie down, Signor Polsinelli."

Abandoned.

I'll wait a bit before leaving the procession. Inside my head I've already left it. I'm not there any more. I carry on walking like a zombie. Exhausted.

Disappointed.

Don't hold this against me, Dario.

It was a great idea, but it's already long forgotten. I wanted to do it for you, in your memory. And for me, too. And for my father. He would have really loved it. He likes anything that turns things upside down a bit. He would have been proud of us, come to think of it . . .

All of a sudden there's a commotion. People are pushing past me. I come back down to earth, right there next to them. The procession snakes in every direction to disperse as if overrun by panic. Up ahead I can hear dozens of people shouting.

"*Fuoco! Fuoco!*"

I look up.

Fire . . .

Yes, fire . . . The mob scatters off the road and onto my land, I'm carried along with them. Fire . . . they've seen the fire . . . As if I still can't believe it I grab the first person I can by the sleeve, and ask him what's going on.

"Well, look right there, *porca miseria*! Look!"

The crowd is shouting and heading towards the vineyard. By standing on tip-toe I can see at last . . .

A ball of flame. Alone, right in the middle of the plot. Good and round. Magnificent. I don't have to do anything. Just stay there. Keep still in this wave of panic. And admire the whirling flames.

Someone in the distance is shouting into the megaphone, saying it's already too late. That nothing can be done to save the chapel.

It burns so quickly. A few men busy themselves, trying no one knows quite what in an attempt to check

113

the blaze. But they very soon give up and watch, powerless, as the belly of the fire completely consumes the building.

The cries die down too and the whole crowd stays standing, frozen, hypnotized by the spectacle. The population of Sora leaving a part of its history to burn.

In a few minutes the whole chapel will collapse. What can they all be thinking, these two thousand or so villagers who've all heard the story of this dump from one generation to the next? There they stand, silently. Ashamed, perhaps, some of the older ones. Ashamed of having let it fall into disrepair. It had already been dead for years.

Suddenly, the first cracking sounds. Quiet muttering spreads through the assembly. They're waiting, feeling oddly moved, their hearts beating, they want to see. The flames have reached right over the dome. The fire took so quickly, it went for it hammer and tongs; the little ruined chapel is a tasty morsel, a sweet that you lick one minute and then swallow whole. Absolutely no resistance. Quite the opposite, in fact, complete abandon. One long flame rises very high. Another crack. I stand open-mouthed, my arms hanging by my sides. Like everyone else, waiting for the inevitable.

The crowd shrank back rapidly when the walls began to give.

Then the two side walls both collapsed at once. They gave way and fell outwards as if they'd been pulled, not imploding and crumbling inside the building. The dome rolled away behind it. The chapel opened out like a flower and at that moment the crowd cried out.

The walls lay down on the ground and the fire spread out around them for a few seconds before losing all its intensity.

And then.

In the middle of the flames and the black smoke, when it all seemed to be over . . .

The Saint appeared to us.

Standing upright on his stone plinth.

Intact.

His eyes looking more implacable than ever.

Sant'Angelo stared at the crowd.

A woman beside me lowered her head and covered her eyes.

There he is amongst the still crackling remains, he is still standing, quite whole, and not even the tiniest little flame has dared to defy him.

His body has a strange sheen to it.

In the front few rows a little group of men steps back.

A woman has fainted, she is carried off, without a murmur.

A few dozen feet away from me a couple have just got down on their knees.

The smoke is dissipating and the blaze is in its dying throes. Silence returns, gently, and chills us all the more. Sant'Angelo, now open to the four winds, Sant'Angelo in all his glory looks down on us miserable sinners. That's how we all see him, every one of us.

Me too.

I've forgotten everything.

A moment – or an eternity – later someone wanted to break the silence. A madman. He walked over towards the statue like a puppet with one arm raised in front of him, and a woman near me brought her hand up to her chest. Very slowly, he reached the plinth.

Sant'Angelo is shiny, streaming with something.

The man hesitated for a moment, as if afraid of being burned.

Then he touched him.

His hand stroked him for a moment. He turned round, incredulous, his eyes open wide, and said:

"*E vino . . .*"

There was a rush of whispering as the word spread right to the back.

"*E vino! E vino!*"

"It's wine!" Yes, it's wine. Sant'Angelo is streaming with wine, sweating and weeping wine. His wine.

Women and children scream, men jostle, pushing too hard. The man who touched the saint drops to the ground. Someone else goes to help him.

And then from nowhere a harrowing wail overlaid everything else. A human wail. A man.

A circle formed around him. I wanted to get as close as I could; quite violently, I pushed aside anyone in my way, so as not to miss one snippet. The man's on his knees, still groaning.

He's lying prostrate with the palms of his hands flat up against his face.

No one dares to go and help him. Out of fear. I want to see. He's still wailing and sobbing like a child.

It's Marcello.

He crawls towards the statue on his knees and elbows. People stand aside for him, he's crying more and more loudly. His way is clear, he covers the muddy ground and finally reaches the plinth. From the crowd the cry goes up: "*Lo cieco . . . lo cieco!*" Yes, it's the blind man all right, suffering like a martyr at the saint's feet. He cries out one last time, his hands haven't left his face. He turns round on himself and falls to the ground, spent.

A cloak of perfect silence descends on us all.

Marcello stays motionless for a long while. Then, slowly, his hands slide from his face and fall to the ground.

He lifts up his head. Looks at the sky. Then looks at us.

His eyes are wide open.

He turns to look at the saint and holds out his arms to him. Then he falls back down, as if he were dead.

An elderly man goes over to him and shakes him. Marcello pushes him aside sharply.

"Don't touch me . . . Don't touch me!"

I push right through to the front. Marcello stares at us for a moment in silence, and then turns back to the saint.

"My eyes . . .! My eyes are burning . . . Sant' Angelo . . . And I can see you . . ."

His eyes weep as they turn to the crowd.

"I can see you . . . all of you!"

Nine in the evening.

In the early afternoon you could still just about count them. In less than an hour the news spread to the surrounding villages and all the people who should have been going to the Gonfalone flocked here. Two thousand, then three thousand, then five thousand souls. Some have knelt down, others stand in silence with joined hands, some make comments, describing it for those who've just arrived, others pace round anxiously. The *fiera* didn't happen that year. But no one's lost out in the deal, they're all getting ready for a different sort of sleepless night.

Sant'Angelo is back.

Daylight is fading already. The refreshment stalls have moved here, people can eat and drink. The local TV station was here by midday to capture the first images. Then the people from RAI came in the early evening to be sure of having live coverage for the *Telegiornale* at eight o'clock.

I kept one eye on the crew's monitor and the other on the journalist, in flesh and blood, microphone askew, just a hundred and fifty feet from the crumbled remains. Oddly enough, it was thanks to the little screen that I grasped the true nature of the event, as if everything that had happened there so far had been a shapeless dream, as if we see things better when they're shown to us. The presenter's clinical account of the events, the close-up on the saint's face and on

118

the charred ruins, the cut-in shots of people kneeling, the reactions of the "witnesses of the miracle" . . .

Miracolo . . .

It was a long wait before that word was unleashed. It took a real pro like the presenter from the RAI to try and tell the whole of Italy about what had just happened here. After mentioning the saint's first apparition in 1886, he held his microphone to a witness, saying: "This morning, Sant'Angelo showed himself again." The old peasant's face looked implacably honest as he waved his arms.

"At first there was a ball of fire . . .", he formed a sphere with his ten fingers and opened his palms, ". . . the chapel split in two, like this . . . like an egg-shell . . ."

I thought fleetingly of Bianca, riveted by her television.

A little further away a handful of men in suits are discussing the technical side of things. Intrigued, I go over to them. Why didn't the dome collapse onto the sculpture, why the thin film of wine? They're all talking at the same time, voices lowered, then stop, for no apparent reason.

I'd so like to come to their help, just to show off, to show them a sketch of the line of the crack which split the chapel in two, and all the strategic points on the building and on the main beam which burned first to ensure that it didn't implode. But the sketches went up in smoke too, in the ashtray in my bedroom. Or, because I'm feeling so exultant, to explain to them what little I learned in Rome about fireproofing processes for wood. But I buried the aerosol can under fifteen feet of soil, somewhere in the vineyard. As for the wine which seeped from Sant'Angelo's body, I could tell them a thing or two about that too. Starting with everything I read about the technical details of miracles which have been in the news in the last few years. Church doors burning spontaneously, icons exuding olive oil, statues of Christ and Santa Lucia weeping, pious images bleeding, and you can even have combinations of the two, busts weeping tears of blood. Why then shouldn't our Sant'Angelo come back amongst us a century later, protected by the wine that he himself asked for and which nobody else gives a damn about . . .

My eyes are on the move the whole time, gauging every kind of reaction. The priest from Sora, Don Nicola, is much in demand. He's accompanied by two young seminarians, and people want to shake his hand, he's asked to speak but he apparently really doesn't want to. Off-screen the RAI presenter groans when his assistant comes to tell him that, despite various attempts and hours of negotiations, the one witness they really want to talk to has definitively refused to be interviewed. The camera comes back to him: "Still under the effects of the shock, Signor Marcello Di Palma has chosen to leave the site, but I have with me someone close to him who witnessed the moment when his sight was restored."

"Oh Marcello, everyone knows Marcello, he's a local figure, he's been living on charity for years . . . His eyes, they're a family illness, his father . . . good soul that he was . . . he had the illness too . . . I remember the old man, Marcello and I are the same age, you see . . . and Marcello lost his sight too, like his father, when he was twelve or thirteen. . . or thereabouts . . ."

This "someone close to him" is struggling to express himself in a patois which is hermetically inaccessible to at least half the nation. All you can tell is that he's making prodigious efforts not to use the word "blind" when he talks about Marcello. I already know the blind man's story well, and better than anyone born and raised with him.

In fact he hasn't chosen to leave the site at all, a corner of the barn has been cleared for him so that he can come to terms with things a bit. Only the doctor and Don Nicola have visited him since his state of grace. There are plans for him to undergo psychological and medical tests in a few days' time. But, whether or not people like it, there's no denying the evidence. He can see.

The journalist went off the air, then came on again quarter of an hour later, and the first image on the monitor was a vine.

One of my vines, on TV . . .

The guy's voice, off: "Any minute now we're hoping to hear from the man who tends these vines and has been making Sant'Angelo's wine for several years . . ."

Ah yes, good old Giacomo . . . I'd forgotten about him. I don't know how well he'll cope with a microphone, given that he always looks at his feet when he's talking and only ever opens his mouth to say he's sorry.

I carry on walking through this giant *tableau vivant*, like a sort of Giotto-style, post-apocalyptic fresco. People sitting, people kneeling, groups of men speaking with their hands over their mouths. The earth scuffed and churned up in places. The encroaching dusk, a few points of bright light, candles or torches, I don't know. And all the rest of it, everything we can't see but which weighs heavily on our shoulders, a silence that's come down from on high, the chilling presence of the irrational, the reverence of believers, the waiting of sceptics, the fear that something else might happen. Who knows? Because it's faith that

121

makes miracles. Without the faithful and their will to believe, nothing would have happened.

Every now and then someone in the crowd points me out discreetly to their friends. And I could have predicted that too. I can almost hear them: "*That bloke over there, that's him, he owns the vineyard . . . He's French. He's the son of some old boy from Sora who lives in Paris . . . Sant'Angelo's wine belongs to him too. Yup. Him alone . . .* Ammazza!"

What about you, Dario? What do think about it? It's just as you planned it, isn't it? We went through it all a thousand times, the two of us, didn't we? I hope you can see all this from where you are. Because you set the whole thing up, after all, this whole epic production. When I think of everything I had to go through to interpret your messages from beyond the grave, my God . . . You could have made it a bit clearer with your "*il miracolo si svolgera*". And the miracle did come to pass. But there were plenty of others before this one, little miracles that were just mine, apparitions I alone saw, revelations that no one will ever know about. You really stitched everyone up saying you wanted to get closer to the land, your mother and Madame Raphaëlle bought it hook, line and sinker. Now, that would have been a miracle, seeing you bent double under a basket of grapes one October morning. I'm proud I smelled a rat right from the start. But I have to admit that the finale was pretty impressive.

The TV truck has packed up and left. Families are heading back to the village, but there are groups of inquisitive people arriving by the carload from all over the place. Amongst them there are some true pilgrims who have come to move in where the villagers have left, tired and done out of their *fiera*. A quick glance at Sant'Angelo would cost dear if you could put a price on it. Thinking along the same lines, the shy Giacomo came to see me just after his television interview. I knew why before he even opened his mouth, but I played the innocent. Today, I made this man go through something which will turn his quiet life upside down.

"Signor Polsinelli, everyone's asking me about the wine . . . The people selling refreshments would really like to buy a bit off us, they said. So, you see, I don't know what to do. And I'm going to give you the key to the barn."

"With everything that's happened today, I can't face dealing with this, Giacomo. Maybe tomorrow . . ."

"But . . . *padrone*. There really are a lot of them, a lot of them asking for it . . . Do you realize, *padrone* . . . I'm sure we could sell a dozen vats just like that. Perhaps twice that . . ."

He moved closer to my ear. The innocent glow in his eyes has evaporated just like that, too. For ever, perhaps.

"And we could even charge another 1,000 lira a bottle. It would still go."

"Do you think so?"

"I'm sure. Even 2,000."

A sort of hypocritical sense of decency stopped me from sniggering. So the shy gentleman turns out to be a prodigy in mental arithmetic. The same man who, just yesterday, would have given a barrel of the wine away to anyone who wasn't rude about it. Actually, that suits me quite well. I've found my business manager. He can do the rest of it for himself, I just have to show him the way.

"For tonight, we won't touch the vats in the cellar, but I think there's a barrel left just by the entrance to the barn. You sort out the price . . ."

He thanks me with a quick nod, and skidaddles off to his barrel.

I can hear a great wave of whispering surging up, tongues are wagging in every corner. A moment of tension. In the distance I can see the doctor making his way through the crowd.

"There's a woman who's not feeling very good, she's feeling faint . . ."

I hadn't thought this would happen. To tell the truth I'd given up hope it would. After reading as many reports as I could on the subject, I find that particular phenomenon perfectly explicable. Predictable, even. The nervous tension, tiredness, the climate, feelings of faith, the crowd, an accumulation of factors which gives certain more fervent individuals a feeling close to intense desire. A shooting pain, a sudden sense of well-being, and the impressionable subject can drop like a stone. In this instance it is indeed a woman with a strong faith who hasn't left the place since early this morning. She passed out after having violent cramps in her arms and legs. She is carried to the ambulance. Nothing miraculous has happened to her. But her fainting fit has put the buzz back into the crowd. The tiniest sign is all it takes to perpetuate the desire to believe.

But I'm actually beginning to feel tired.

I went and ate a grilled lamb chop and drank a beer. I'm shivering a bit in my thin shirt. What wouldn't I give to go back to Bianca's house and watch all this from an armchair on Radio Tele Sora, in the warmth!

Giacomo's looking for me everywhere, and finds me. He's almost in tears and wonders how I can stay so calm in all this.

"I can't hold out any longer, *padrone* . . . They're going to break the place down if I don't open another vat . . . this evening. I could sell the lot . . . the lot!"

124

"You can sell the lot tomorrow."

"But why wait till tomorrow? Just with what was there I've made, I daren't even tell you what I've made, *padrone* . . ."

He hands me a wad of banknotes. Without really knowing why, I looked away.

"Keep it all, Giacomo . . . But keep it safe."

"What do you mean, *padrone*?"

There was a moment's silence. Then I asked him whether he had a sweater or something warm in the barn. He said something about an old jacket. I thanked the heavens for it.

It's going to be a long night.

There were seven of them yesterday, and I only managed to put three of them off. The others set off at full speed first thing this morning, and reached the vineyard before me. Sant'Angelo only came back into work ten days ago, and I'm already crumbling under the daily onslaughts of these guys who keep appearing from all over Italy, laden with dodgy business propositions and crooked contracts.

"Signor Polsinelli! Have you thought about the offer I made yesterday?"

"Say, Signor Polsinelli, you're going to have to give it an *appellation controlée!*"

"Can we talk for a minute, Signor Polsinelli? Have you thought about exporting? Next stop Europe, watch out!"

"I'll buy thirty feet back from you! Just thirty feet! Name your price!"

I'm being offered all sorts of things, starting with simply selling the whole lot, increasing the production four- or five-fold, untold different labels . . . Two blokes wearing ties even came to blows, I watched them.

At first there were just wine merchants, people who produced, marketed and sold plonk. They were joined by a cohort of people who wanted to create pious pictures and a great diversity of knickknacks in the image of Sant'Angelo. They want to build a row of little kiosks on the edge of the property. They wouldn't have to cut down any vines. All I need do is pick up the rent in the high season. I don't know what to think about it.

I was very soon snowed under. Luckily for me, some kind of accountant who looks a bit like Lucky Luciano came to offer me his services three days after the miracle. Giacomo immediately nicknamed him the *dottore* because of his little glasses, his diplomas and his obstinate refusal to smile. He's a gem. He looks at every single proposal and deals with the meetings. When he shows me his notes with calculations in every direction, they look like Garigliano's battle plans.

And yet the sums had been quite simple in my little head. Only, that was before they came. And just in my little head. The 30,000 unsold litres at 50 francs a 75cl bottle would give 12 million francs. With an income of about 500,000 francs a year, after expenses. With that, I could stop everything and put myself out to pasture for the rest of my days. But since these businessmen in every flavour have been turning up, my stupid little sums have fallen by the wayside.

Giacomo's become the consummate foreman. He's taken on six men to prepare for the next harvest. In the meantime, one of them is in charge of meeting and greeting pilgrims (of which there are an average of three hundred a day). Another manages the parking. Another deals with retail sales on the basis of one and only one bottle per person per day. Giacomo oversees the building work: the masons who have only just finished the little recess to protect Sant'Angelo for centuries to come, the restoration of the statue by a specialist from Milan, direct access to the sacred place along a tarmacked track, and the layout of electric fences around the plot. I spend my days organizing this whole circus, listening to offers from these good people, and keeping a tally of expenses with the *dottore* who wields his calculator like a machine-gun. Bianca wakes me at six each morning and sees me come back at about eleven o'clock at night, exhausted, harassed and starving hungry. A few of the really predatory ones have rented rooms in her house and abuse the situation by hounding me right into my own room to get me to sign stuff when the *dottore* isn't looking. That's how I realized the guy was indispensable.

Sora has become a centre for pilgrims and the downright curious. Trade is very brisk, and the restaurants and hotels are full to bursting. Some have changed their names: one trattoria has been renamed "Sant'Angelo's Table", and there's a "Vineyard Hotel". But they have a funny way of looking at me when I come back in the evenings. Maybe they resent me for shaking up the end of their summer.

The mayor came to invite me to a meeting of the local council, and I couldn't understand why. The solicitor has asked me to stop by at his office to go over some details. As I cross the market place someone taps me on the shoulder to congratulate me with a forced laugh; some old boy has come to tell me that he knew my father back in the days when he had his turkeys; another tried to pass himself off as a distant cousin; some fifteen year-old girls whistled when I passed them; some kids on scooters tried to spit on me. Everyone calls me *lo straniero*. The foreigner. I've always been told that an immigrant will be a foreigner wherever he goes, and I'm beginning to understand it. But in this case it's a foreigner who's made their own land yield a profit. I can feel an atmosphere building up around me, and day after day Bianca asks me to take care.

But all this is small fry compared to what happened the very first day after the miracle. That's when I was really rattled.

At the request of the Bishop of the Diocese of Frosinone, the Vatican opened a file and sent two emissaries to study the phenomenon on site. Standard procedure. I knew they would come, I was almost waiting for them. But I couldn't have guessed what was going to step out of the Lancia Thema registered in the Vatican State.

Two unexploded bombs in civilian clothes. These guys were as silent and serious as if they'd just been excommunicated, they were polite and discreet, with every ounce of determination they needed to get right to the job. As soon as they set foot on the land, the crowds of faithful parted like the Red Sea before Moses. That was when I understood that the joke was well and truly over. For a good week they searched through the ashes, looking for God knows what with equipment which became more sophisticated by the day. Without uttering one superfluous word, without making any attempt to talk to Giacomo or myself. Two ice-cool sleuths ferreting through the charred stones and sniffing the statue from head to foot. Two nuncios who looked for all the world like private detectives concentrating on their enigma, silent like real pros, trying to find the telling mistake, doubting everything, even the evidence. Seeing them poking around like that, I could feel they wanted to find a culprit. They made enquiries about Marcello round the village. The doctor who came to join them ran tests on him for two days. No one could get to talk to him for forty-eight hours.

Did you know all this would happen, Dario? No, of course not, you hadn't pictured any of the consequences of your luminous idea. And now you couldn't give a damn, could you? You didn't even know guys like them existed, did you?

The other three didn't arrive till this morning. In a Mercedes 600, also registered at the Vatican, which they parked right by the vineyard. Three passengers, one chauffeur. Only one of them got out of the car, accompanied by a young priest who acted as his secretary. The two emissaries who were hanging about nearby scrambled back to work the minute they saw this purple shadow coming slowly over to the statue of the protector. There was almost a riot in which a great crowd of pilgrims rushed over to him. Don Nicola went absolutely white. They all knelt to kiss his glove. Then they talked for almost an hour, in the car, and no one was allowed to get anywhere near them. A long time later the secretary came over to introduce me to the bishop.

I didn't know how to behave. I put one knee on the ground before his robes as they gleamed in the sunlight. Oddly enough, it was when I touched his glove that I realized it had all gone too far, and that sooner or later I would end up in prison.

A mass?

Yes, they're going to celebrate mass the day after tomorrow, in the morning, here, out in the open. An official mass. Celebrated by the bishop. It's traditional. The secretary and Don Nicola will take care of everything. No harm will come to the land.

"It's too precious to us, wouldn't you say, Monsignor?" asked the secretary, smiling at his boss.

The whole time this conversation was going on, I kept one eye on the silhouette which stayed seated in the Mercedes. And which only deigned to come out once I'd set off along the path to leave the place.

* * *

On my way back I met Mangini with his shotgun over his arm. I could see rabbit feet hanging from his pouch. He abandoned his polite third person singular for a more colloquial *tu* form. He seemed worried, edgy even.

"Don't let all this get to you, Antonio. I've seen all these people hanging about, priests and people making you promises. Don't let them pull the wool over your eyes, that's all I'll say. Can you see the lights over there behind the trees? That's where I live. I just wanted to let you know . . . and I don't know why I'm telling you . . . but if you need some advice . . . if you want somewhere to hide . . . you can come any time."

I didn't try to understand. I just held out my hand. He opened his arms and held me to him.

As I went over the Naples bridge, I saw a line of Vespas parked along the terrace of the last café in Sora that was still open. A gang of young lads sprawled in orange plastic chairs broke off their rowdy conversation the minute they saw me coming. A few moments of deathly silence as I walked past them. Then, without looking back, I heard a concert of kick-starts. Very soon the Vespas were circling and backfiring round me, trying to brush past me and block my way. The boys were all laughing, calling me *stronzo, disgrazziato* and all sorts of other names. I walked a little faster, regretting that I didn't have Mangini's gun, the only thing that could have redressed the balance of power. A little youngster with curly hair managed to slap me on the nape of the neck as he accelerated past me, and I wasn't able to retaliate quickly enough. As I walked on I could see shutters being closed and doors being opened a fraction in the darkness.

"What do you want, you bunch of morons?" I yelled.

They stopped some thirty feet from me. I crossed

the street, and they turned back towards the other pavement. This game went on for a while. I don't know exactly what they want, they probably don't either. They just want to annoy me, out of jealousy, as a form of revenge. I've engendered a general feeling of irritation in the town, and I should have expected that too. Only the young are daring to air their feelings at the moment, and even then it's only when there are ten of them together in the middle of the night. One who is probably bolder than the rest blocks my way and looks me up and down sardonically.

Over the last few days, I've really been beginning to feel tired. It's time I got home to bed.

"Hey, you, you little show-off, if you want me to get out of your pitiful town, get out of my way . . ."

He turned to the others and bellowed what I had said at the top of his lungs. They all imitated me in chorus, taking care to accentuate my incorrect pronunciation.

"You're not leaving, are you?" the ringleader said with a laugh. "But we like you too much to let you leave, *ammazza*!"

He was balancing on his scooter, and I made the most of the fact that he had turned to laugh with the others to deliver him a healthy blow which toppled him to the ground. I started running to Bianca's house to the accompaniment of screaming engines.

Completely out of breath, I slammed shut the outside door, and they hammered on it for a long time before giving up. Bianca was trembling.

"Do you want me to go and sleep somewhere else?" I asked.

"It's not me I'm worried about, Antonio . . ."

She didn't wake me until about nine o'clock. She probably thought I needed the sleep.

"You can take your time, Antonio. The *dottore* came by to say he'd deal with this morning's meetings."

Just hearing those words made me feel like going back to bed.

"A man from the Red Cross came to ask you for a donation. I told him he could go to Sant'Angelo!"

They want me dead. All of them. I don't know whether Dario would have held out any longer than me. I switch the TV on, it's time for the programme. Bianca settles herself between two cushions.

The *Chronicle of Miracles*, on RAI, ten minutes of a sort of hit parade giving all the news of religious events and miraculous phenomena across the country. Today: an apparition in Sicily, a little piece on the Turin Shroud, which is being carbon-dated, with Bach as background music, and then they switch to Sant'Angelo with the umpteenth resumé of the facts relating to the miracle and an announcement about the mass the bishop will be holding tomorrow. A really big event, the commentator said.

I'd thought of everything. Except for the purple. Bianca is delighted and can't think why I'm not equally enthusiastic.

Now the journalist comes to the topic I've been waiting for, a pre-recorded interview with the man "miraculously cured in the vineyard".

I was there when they filmed it, they asked for my permission to film in the barn. Marcello was perfect. Bianca gives a little squeak of excitement as soon as she sees him on the screen.

"It's so difficult to describe ... I heard people shouting about the fire, I could feel the panic everywhere, and I was frightened. No one bothered to explain to me ... then there was the silence. And I started to feel strange ... a burning feeling starting in my stomach and rising up slowly ... then, there was the light ..."

Calm. Serene. Almost motionless. Apart from his dialect which you could cut with a knife, there was nothing left of the character who used to make the whole region laugh and sing.

People have learned to use his actual name ... Last time we spoke to each other, six days after the miracle, he was about to head north to blow the 20 million lira I'd promised him from the first profits from selling the stock.

"I was fed up with those glasses, Antonio. And thanks to you I was able to chuck them in the gutter ... Begging didn't suit me at my age."

I didn't understand why there was that little note of nostalgia in his voice. Perhaps he wanted to say exactly the opposite. Perhaps he too suddenly felt like an orphan. You can't just put forty years of work behind you like that.

"My mother, now she was a real saint ... My father was already blind when she married him, and no one expected anything from the poor guy, all he was good for was holding his hand out."

They have a child. He can see, and that's the best thing that could happen to Signora Di Palma. But times are hard for everyone after the war, and how's a blind man going to join in the waves of people emigrating? The father teaches his son music, how to play the banjo and the accordion, and the two of them do the circuit of weddings, parties and baptisms in the region.

"As soon as someone was organizing a party, me and my old man would set off, walking for a good two days to Roccasecca, Arpino, all those little places . . . It was going quite well, people liked us and we put our hearts into it."

The mother dies of pneumonia when Marcello is ten. The father and son become complete nomads. They work in market places and as people are coming out of church.

"We had our calendar, and Sundays – I don't need to tell you – were the best days of the week, especially in winter. We would sing Pagliaccio and Funiculi funicula, opera arias and folk songs. The one time the old boy was ill I just had to work on my own. So I put his glasses on, just to see how it went, in some back of beyond place where they didn't know us. And when the old boy realized that I hadn't done badly, well, that's when the idea came to him."

The father goes round telling everyone about the hereditary disease that affects them both. Two blind men can make more money than one. Marcello takes to wearing glasses.

"My father would say: 'We've got the evil eye, it's handed from father to son!' and people would stop laughing then. I learned how to be blind – the stick, how to move, especially head movements – and no one ever noticed anything."

Marcello is twenty-four when his father dies, and the only thing he can do is play music. He's known everywhere, he's well liked, it's his life.

"What could I do? I didn't have anything better to go to anywhere else. I carried on, on my own. I even forgot I could see, I wasn't even ashamed any longer. When I could feel people watching me pityingly, I closed my eyes . . . it was as good as."

One day he decides to restrict his field of action, and to concentrate on the area round Sora.

"That was where I felt happiest, I was a part of the village. I knew that if I stayed in Sora there would be no question of seeing again. People would have lynched me if they'd known I was abusing their charity. That's only natural, isn't it? And the good thing about here was this barn, which no one ever tried to stop me sleeping in, and the wine which no one ever tried to stop me drinking, because no one else wanted it. Might as well let the blind man make the most of it . . ."

One day Dario became the landowner. No one knew what he wanted, what he was up to.

"It's handy when you can read someone's thoughts when they don't know they're being watched. When I saw that one I knew straight away he had some funny ideas. There it is . . . we didn't know each other for long, that French boy and me, but I can tell you no one'll ever see a schemer like that one again . . . He was a funny guy, a bit crafty, a bit of liar. A bit like me, really . . ."

Dario doesn't drive him out, quite the opposite. He gets into the habit of coming over late in the evening and drinking with the blind man.

"He asked me things about the village, about the vineyard and Sant'Angelo. He was the first person who'd ever asked me about my own life. He would keep on offering me drink until I was completely drunk. Sneaky bugger . . . I trusted him. Then one day, I don't remember when, but I was pissed out of my brain and I did something unnatural, for a blind person, I mean . . . I gave myself away, and that bloody fool didn't miss any of it. He told me he'd guessed as much. I said he was crafty . . ."

What a godsend, a fake blind man. No question of backtracking after making a discovery like that.

"And that was when he suddenly said one evening: 'How much do you make with your begging and busking? Not much, is it? I'll buy you out and you can close down the business . . . 20 million lira in cash and an income for life indexed to the price of the wine. Aren't you fed up with being blind . . .?'"

Marcello doesn't resist for long. Being an actor for a few days, telling a few tall stories, improvising, no problem, that's what he does. But there is the slight worry about reintegrating into society, living with others, like others.

"Look people in the eye? Me? Do you think I'd be able to after so many years? But at the same time the idea's just too beautiful: having the right to see again and, at the same time, taking it easy with a real packet for the rest of my days."

They put together a plan. Dario chooses the day of the Gonfalone to ensure as many witnesses as possible, and they rehearse the sequence of events. Then he goes back to Paris. Never to return.

"The day I heard he was dead I thought it must be a sign from God. And I wrote my song. He'd made me want to see with my own eyes again, that's what he called it. It was too wonderful. I had to choose between leaving the country and going quietly back to my life as a beggar with the people I knew. I made my choice. I wouldn't have lasted long anywhere else, even with my eyesight. Then one evening you came along . . ."

We fell into each others arms a bit before he left.

"You made me do something pretty strange, Antonio. How did I think I was going to live like everyone else after this? No one thinks of me as a blind man any more, but as someone who's been cured by a miracle. I don't know which is worse. I went from darkness into light too quickly, you know . . . the doctor representing the Church, the one who wouldn't get off my back for two days, thought I was a peculiar creature. They were pretty suspicious, him and his two henchmen from the Vatican. They don't like this sort of thing, you know . . ."

I didn't want to go over it again, but he was wrong. It's been established that the most plausible and most frequent cases of spontaneous recovery are from blindness and some forms of paralysis. After a violent shock people can recover their sight or the use of their limbs. The Medical Records Office at Lourdes has acknowledged dozens of cases without hailing them as miracles.

"And if I stay here I know they'll look at me like that all my life. And I was the one who didn't want to move somewhere new . . . I feel hounded . . . people want to touch me, to tell me about their problems, and I wear myself out telling them I haven't got any gift, I haven't got anything, but they want to see me anyway. People in the village no longer laugh when they see me. The old woman who used to give me meat wanted to kiss my hand . . . I'm ashamed, more ashamed than when I used to see the world through my glasses."

"Don't say that, Marcello . . ."

"I haven't even got the heart to add another couplet to my song. Who would I sing it to? I've got my sight back but I've lost my voice."

"Do you regret it?"

"No, not really . . . It's only been a few days and I'm already getting a taste for sleeping in a bed. I'm getting old. Yesterday a lad from *la Gazetta* asked me some questions for his paper. He asked me what it was like seeing a rainbow. I told him it was wonderful but I couldn't tell whether or not I was lying."

"What are you going to do?"

"Nothing. Wait for a while before coming back here. Travel. See things. Watch things. Florence, Venice.

Don't forget to send me the money, anything that's beautiful is expensive."

He packed his things without really knowing how to go about it. The very idea of a suitcase was a problem for him. I asked him one last time whether he understood why Dario had been killed.

"I don't know who did that. I can't help you there. But when you've got twisted ideas like that in your head . . ."

He left on the last train so that he would meet as few people as possible. It would be as well for us not to be seen together. I didn't go with him.

Bianca switches the television off and shakes my shoulder gently.

"Don't go back to sleep, they're waiting for you there."

She smiles, kindly. Would she let me share her bed if she suspected I was a swindler, a cheat and a hypocrite?

While she's getting ready to go to the market she leans out of the window. Her white petticoat hangs down well below her knees. She giggles.

But her attention is suddenly drawn to one end of the street. Outside I can hear the purr of a very smooth engine. A few bursts of conversation. And a melodious sequence of slamming doors. Bianca looks back towards me for a moment, visibly excited, and she tries to say something with her hands.

"It's . . . it's *Dallas*, Antonio! Come and look! No . . . it's not *Dallas* . . . it's *Miami Vice*!"

Ouch . . .

I don't understand what she means. But I can already tell it'll hurt.

I go over to the window slowly. The commotion out in the street is getting louder. The sun's already blazing down. It's going to be a long day.

Down below: two white Cadillacs with tinted windows. Just as you would imagine them. Even longer and shinier. The local Fiats have slipped away like mice to let them park along the whole length of the pavement. Little kids have clustered round, old boys are coming out to have a closer look. Bianca's quivering.

"It's just like the one Sue Ellen's Californian lover drives."

This apparition is on a par with Sant'Angelo's. I try and forget about the cars themselves to eye up who's stepped out of them. Not difficult. Three white men and a black man. It's this last one who's a real hit with the crowd. Have they ever actually seen one before in this godforsaken place? His hair is close shaven and he's wearing a shiny grey suit and a white shirt. The others are wearing glasses and lamé suits. The biggest of the four takes a briefcase from the boot of the car and hands it to the only one in the group with a beard. At the moment it's impossible to tell which is the boss. A group of jostling children have pressed up against one of the doors to try and make out every detail of the interior. There are adults snooping round the number plates, touching the bodywork and talking loudly. The bearded one and the black man clap their hands twice, extraordinarily slowly. The crowd shuffles back fifteen feet. A third man bursts out laughing. The bearded one takes out a big white handkerchief and rubs a tiny area of the windscreen.

Leaden silence.

One of them takes off his Ray-Bans and wipes his forehead with his sleeve. Then he heads slowly for the nearest café, and starts talking to the manager who's joined the crowd of onlookers. Impossible to hear what they're saying. People are bowing in front of him, chairs are being moved aside, but the guy with the

Ray-Bans refuses to sit down. After a couple of minutes the barman seems to realize what's being asked of him, he tilts his head up and looks searchingly at the building opposite. He smiles rather awkwardly. Then he raises his arm and points towards our window. The four visitors turn their heads towards me.

*   *   *

Two sharp raps on the door. Haven't had time to react or even get dressed. Or prepare any sort of defence. I don't even know what form the attack will take. It's a paranoid reaction, but how could I fail to be paranoid with this truck-load of problems bearing down on me? Protect me, Sant'Angelo, you owe me that at least. The people of Sora can enjoy a good show, worthy of the big screen in the cinema they've lost. Just as it used to be, with seats in the stalls and a bit of clowning around on the screen before the main feature.

"Shall I open the door?" Bianca asks me.

"Yes."

The four men come in, the one with the Ray-Bans asks where I am. The others sniff about round the kitchen, I can hear their voices. Bianca's right, they talk like characters in one of those badly dubbed American soaps, especially when they snigger, it's not violent or exaggerated, but it pins you to your seat. The black one takes the lid off a casserole and breathes in deeply. The guy with the Ray-Bans isn't pleased.

"Put that back, you jerk."

He puts it back, grumbling.

The man with the Ray-Bans seems to be the boss.

He holds out his hand to me.

"Polsinelli?"

"Yes."

"Parini. Giuseppe Parini. Does the name mean anything to you . . .?"

He chews his words, massacres them. The drawling accent of an American who can't even speak his own language and is having a go at Dante's. Of course I know who you are. You owned two and a half acres of the vineyard. You've got a chain of laundrettes in New Jersey. You're a cousin of the Cuzzos.

Probably in his fifties, with a nose that's a bit too big for his gaunt cheeks, a smile which doesn't stay the course for very long and – particularly, most particularly – a little gleam in his eye which implies that he likes to keep chit-chat to a minimum. However hard he tries to pass himself off as an American, something gives him away. He's got the stamp of the wop about him in spite of himself.

The bearded one sits down on the sofa, another henchman sits astride a chair with a match between his teeth.

"Hasn't the *ragazza* got work to do?" he says, flicking his thumb at Bianca.

I see. No point in explaining that the *ragazza* in question is in her own home. Bianca has already left. I feel ashamed. But, for the time being, I'd rather let them get on with it than try to teach them a few manners. She's hardly slammed the door before the henchmen start making themselves at home. One switches on the TV, another opens the fridge, the third looks round two or three of the rooms.

I must be dreaming . . .

You can't try to tell me these guys have come to deliver clean laundry. And that their boss has come to spend a weekend in his home country. For nostalgia's sake.

142

"It's great being back here, Polsinelli . . . I'd forgotten how beautiful it was, all this greenery. This is the *dolce vita*. They're lucky, these good people, very lucky."

The black man is tapping his thigh as he watches TV over his friend's shoulder. A repeat of *Kojak*. The boss asks them to be quieter.

"I've heard that things are going very well here . . . Good business . . .?"

His road is pretty long, too. The Italian diaspora has worked well. In less than ten days he's heard about the miracle and he's not lost a minute.

The bearded one helps himself to a few ladlefuls of minestrone, the others giggle like little kids listening to the funny voices dubbed onto familiar actors.

Parini picks up the briefcase and puts it on the table. An attaché-case. I see dozens like it every day, full of good things: contracts, money, promises, income for life. I wait for him to open it to discover what this one has to offer me.

"We're going to do business, aren't we?"

He clicks open the two locks with his thumbs and waits for a moment.

"He was nice, young Trengoni, a real sweet-talker . . . he reeled me in, no problem. But there you have it, Polsinelli. I'm very ashamed of selling this sacred land. I respect the saints, genuinely. But what is signed is signed, I'm a man of my word, Polsinelli. The land's yours now."

I've got it, he wants to go into business with me and to offer me a deal. He's deliberately delaying the moment when he opens the briefcase. I'm full of anticipation, my eyes glued to the leather.

"But I sold it for a song, didn't I? You'd agree with that? And that was sacrilegious. I'm ashamed of myself.

143

Oh, if Sant'Angelo knew that I'd given away his vineyard for a few thousand dollars!"

He raises his arms to the heavens. And opens the briefcase. I open my eyes wide . . .

And see nothing. Absolutely nothing. The briefcase is completely empty.

He claps his hands just once. The others reappear instantly. And stand round me.

"Right, Polsinelli, my business needs me back in New York. Business is business, isn't it? You see this briefcase?"

"Yes . . ."

"I want it full to bursting before this evening. I don't want one little fart of air left in it, do you understand? And, as from today, I want 25 per cent of everything you make from Sant'Angelo. I'll leave two of my men here. If you like you can even choose them, and I recommend Bob, he's a good masseur."

"Wait a minute," I say, smiling, "you're joking . . . For a start I don't have anything in cash and anyway . . ."

Parini cuts me dead.

"If you prefer, there's another way we can fill the case. It's exactly the right volume for a human body your size that's been through Bob's hands for a few minutes. I know from experience, we tried it out last week."

I didn't need a translator when the Bob in question specified, "Without the shoes." All of them pulled my ears, pinched my cheeks and pounded the back of my neck, and they didn't stop until my head had doubled in size.

"You're a good boy, Polsinelli . . . you make a nice couple with the *ragazza*. She's a sweet girl."

"What are you trying to say?"

All four of them pat my shoulders.

144

"You've got until this evening to say yes. It won't be difficult to find us."

"Which . . . which hotel are you in in Sora?"

"Do you really think I'm going to stay in this shitty little arsehole of a place? With all these peasants? We're at the Plane Tree Hotel in Frosinone. But don't worry, we'll know where to find you."

I force myself to laugh. Instead of being sick. They move towards the door. I try to keep them there.

"Tell me, is laundering big in America? I can see now why everyone looks so clean on TV."

The boss translates for the others who burst out laughing and clap their hands.

"Do you have family working in concrete?" I ask Parini.

"Yes."

"And you always travel in a white Cadillac?"

"Yes."

"And you're married to a Sicilian girl?"

"Yes. How do you know all this?"

"I just do. Intuition . . ."

I'd always heard that you had to meet these three conditions to get into *the* big Italian-American family. I just wanted to check.

*　*　*

As I headed towards the vineyard I tried to reason with myself, to persuade myself that this was all a big joke. That, with a bit of goodwill, everything would soon be sorted out. Without managing to convince myself. My shirt's already drenched in sweat, and it's not because of the heat. My face is overrun with nervous tics, I don't know what to do with my hands. Twenty-five per cent for the white Cadillacs? How much for the others? For the Church, for the whole community, for Dario.

A group of tractors backfired behind me. I stood aside on the verge to let them pass, but one of them gave a blast of the raucous hooter which served as a horn, the other three followed suit and I thought my eardrums would burst. The farmers perched behind the steering wheels laughed. One of them veered towards me so that his right-hand wheels were running along the verge, and the others formed a circle round me, weaving in and out in a ballet, imprisoning me with their deafening engines and maddening horns.

I pressed my hands over my ears.

"What the bloody hell have I done to you?" I yelled in French.

Just as two of them bore down on me in a pincer movement I jumped between two wheels and landed in the bottom of a ditch, my face in a pool of insect-ridden muck.

They went on their way. The one bringing up the rear weaved backwards and forwards across the track for a while, and the man called something out to me but I couldn't make out what he was saying.

They want to make me pay. In every sense of the word. Settling up with the entire village? Divine retribution?

But I'm not Dario.

You won't get me.

No one noticed that I was plastered with mud. Nobody gives a damn, even the *dottore* who hardly ever looks up from his figures. He's asked me to have a good look at a proposition from two peasant farmers who own the ten-acre wheat field next to the plot. They're offering to sell it to me at a very elevated price so that I can extend the vineyard. Or at a reasonable price if I give

146

them a cut of the harvests. The *dottore* has already done the sums and is stuffing my head full of percentages, profits and a whole load of other things I couldn't give a flying fuck about. They want to see me dead, and all the calculations in the world can't change that.

The bishop's secretary is overseeing the preparations for the mass with the help of Don Nicola. One of the TV stations is already there. I didn't ask for any of this. I just want to go home.

"Signor Polsinelli, I work for the Red Cross and . . ."

Before he's even finished his sentence I dump him with the *dottore*.

"Signor Polsinelli, I'm the solicitor's clerk, if you would be so kind as to drop by his office as soon as possible . . ."

I say yes, automatically, when I'm actually thinking of far more pressing questions.

"Signor Polsinelli! I'm the designer. Could I show you the sketches for the next label?"

"Signor Polsinelli, I'm a building contractor, I'd like to offer you my services to rebuild your cellars, because . . ."

They want me dead too. I'm going to need another miracle to hold out any longer. Twenty-five per cent for these creeps? I'd rather die, or run away, back to Paris, or anywhere else for that matter, somewhere where nobody knows me, where I'll never be found. I might just set up the first Italian colony in the Galapagos Islands.

But you won't get me.

* * *

At half past four the *dottore* told me what he had worked out. The figures at his fingertips, he had combined the various proposals and was able to double – exactly double – the forecast profits.

"Think about it, Signor Polsinelli."

Think about what? About more shit hitting the fan? Doubling the problems, doubling the blackmail? I left, promising I would look into it.

They won't get me.

I wanted to take a different route, as a precaution, and take the short cut that Marcello had shown me. And then I wondered if that was really a good idea. It was just as I was going past the wheat field that it started raining. Stones. One, then two, skimming past my head. I didn't see anyone. I thought it might be a couple of kids up in a tree. Then there was a whole cloudburst of pebbles above my head. I started to run, and hundreds of stones appeared from every direction. I couldn't see who was throwing them, kids or adults, perched in the trees or crouching among the crops. One stone hit me on the back and I cried out. For a split second I glimpsed a farmer's wife in a white headscarf bending over to pick up more ammunition.

What have I done to them . . .?

They'll have me if I stay one more hour in this place.

I ran so fast I nearly burst a lung. Laying waste to the crops as I went, I reached the town at full pelt, close to asphyxia, with people clapping as I passed, and I didn't slow down until I reached Bianca's house.

She was at her sewing machine in front of the television.

"What's this briefcase here, Antonio?"

I hesitated to tell her that the briefcase might prove as fatal to her as to me.

"I'm leaving or I'm going to die in this place," I said, still hopelessly out of breath.

I must have made quite a sight. Half suffocated, covered in mud and streaming with sweat. Looking like a madman. She took me in her arms.

"Everyone in the village has been asking me about you. Which family you're from, whether you're planning to leave, and when . . ."

"To leave? What time's the last bus to Rome? Quick!"

"At five o'clock."

Ten to, by my watch.

I pulled away from her, probably too harshly, and launched myself into the bedroom where I stuffed my clothes and a few wads of cash into a bag. Bianca didn't say a word. She went back to her work, pretending not to see what I was doing. It suddenly occurred to me that she would never see me again. But fear makes short work of remorse. I hesitated for a second before saying goodbye to her. And I left.

There were thirty or so people on the bus, most of them pilgrims.

"When are we leaving?" I asked the driver, who was sitting idly by the ticket office.

He raised three fingers. I found some empty seats at the back of the bus and threw myself onto them.

Giacomo and the *dottore* will take care of everything. They'll probably cope better without me when it comes to getting the most out of the land. And I'll come back when everyone's calmed down, when the bishop's finished his mass, when his henchmen have finished their enquiry, and when the Americans have gone back to their laundry. I press my cheek against the window to get one last glance of Sora . . .

Everything's calm again.

Apart from the driver who's having a heated discussion with two or three employees from the bus company.

I don't know whether it's my rising paranoia, but I definitely feel as though they're looking at me. They're joined by a couple of local tradesmen – I recognize the barman from the café. They keep looking, sneaking sideways looks at me. I'm probably wrong. I'm going to go mad if I let every suspicion get to me. The three minutes are up. The driver's running late; their conversation starts getting agitated, they're struggling to keep their voices down. I open my window but I still can't hear. The driver's shaking his head, someone takes his arm, shakes him a bit. I don't understand any of it.

Then, suddenly, he's all smiles again for a moment. He gets into the bus but doesn't sit down, and announces to his assembled passengers:

"We've got a bit of engine trouble. It needs sorting out. The bus isn't going to be able to leave now. The company would like to offer its apologies. We'll try and find another bus before the end of the evening. Everybody out!"

The passengers moan, get to their feet, try to argue it out with the driver who just raises his arms in an exaggerated apology.

I stay where I am, dumbly, still gasping, not really taking in what he's just said.

The bastards . . .

They won't get me. I get out and walk past the little group. The barman from the bistro looks away.

You want to hold me down, keep me here, stop me getting away . . . I don't know what it is you're after. But you won't get me.

I round the street corner where the only three taxis in town are usually parked. Someone grabs hold of my arm. I nearly jump out of my skin, ready to punch whoever it is who's trying to hold me back.

"Hey . . . hey! Calm down, Signor Polsinelli! It's me, you do recognize me, don't you?"

It's the solicitor. What the hell's he doing here?

"I've been looking for you everywhere, but you're very difficult to find!"

"Well, everyone else seems to manage! I'm in a hurry, what do you want?"

"I just wanted to tell you that . . . it's rather awkward . . . I may be wrong, but . . ." He moves closer to my ear and glances round furtively.

"I'm bound by professional confidentiality, *signor* . . . but you can't really help leaks . . . I had nothing to do with it, I swear . . . but the whole village now seems to know about . . . the clause . . ."

"What clause?"

"What do you mean, what clause? It's the first thing I talked to you about when you arrived here! The clause which says that, after you, the land reverts in full to the community . . ."

"I don't get it."

"You knew very well that that was what Signor Trengoni wanted. If you were to refuse to accept the land, it would be handed to the entire village. Same thing after your . . . your death."

"Sorry?"

"It's all down on paper. And now that Sant'Angelo has honoured us by returning, and you've made millions out of the vineyard . . ."

A headache is beginning to make my head pound.

"Be careful, Signor Polsinelli . . ."

My legs can barely take my weight, and I lean against the wall.

"Wait a minute . . . wait . . . are you trying to tell me that, in order to get a share in the vineyard, the villagers would be prepared to . . ."

"Oh, I'm not saying anything. I'm just warning you, that's all. So, good luck, then, *signor . . .*"

He leaves me there with a little wave of his hand.

People are crossing over onto the pavement opposite.

The terrace in front of the café is full and absolutely silent.

We like you too much to let you leave . . . that's what that youngster said yesterday.

All these silent faces at the windows.

Motionless.

A taxi appears at the end of the street. I almost throw myself under its wheels. It grinds to a halt.

"Are you crazy?!" bellows the driver.

He doesn't have a passenger. I want to get into the back, but he blocks the door.

In the distance, behind the watermelon lorry, I can see a discreet figure indicating to him that he shouldn't take me.

"I can't, I've got a fare . . ."

I don't know what to do any more, I won't hold out long against this sort of conspiracy. I delve through my bag and take out a nice compact wad of notes. I have no idea what it's worth. "The whole lot if you get me out of town . . ."

He's about to leave but he hesitates at the sight of the money. Then he looks at the group of men coming slowly towards us.

"All right, get in . . ."

He hardly gives me time to climb in before setting off like a madman, and the men yell out in anger.

"Va fan'culooooooo! " shouts the taxi driver, flicking them a V-sign.

He only just misses a couple of pedestrians. People throw things at the bodywork, but the driver doesn't give a damn, and we plough on, straight for the Ponte di Ferro to get out of Sora.

"Are you in trouble, *signor*?" he asks, almost laughing.

"You will be too."

"Me? In trouble? I wouldn't know how to be, I'm from Naples."

His accent confirms it, and so does his driving. The Neapolitans only know a seriously expurgated version of the highway code which can be summed up in one golden rule: "Don't ever stop – or someone'll nick your tyres." The taxi is heading up a little hill; in the distance I can see the waterfall at Isola Liri, a small neighbouring village that you have to go through to get to the county town.

"Now that we're out of there, where are we going?"

"To the station in Frosinone."

"For the money you just showed me, I could take you to Rome, if you like . . ."

Was there that much of it? In all the rush I hadn't had time to count. The taxi slows down.

"What's going on?"

"Look up ahead, *signor* . . . Is that what you call trouble?"

The two Cadillacs are coming slowly towards us. Side by side they are wider than the whole road. The taxi stops.

"Hey . . . is it you these guys are looking for?"

Yup.

"*Porca troia. . .!*"

"What do you mean?"

He stops in front of the two white monsters, and crosses his arms, quite calmly, completely unfazed.

"Turn round, for God's sake! We can't stay here! We can head back towards . . ."

153

"Listen, *signor*, keep your cool, I avoid trouble because I can see it coming. The whole of Sora's chicken feed compared to these four guys. And I'm just a Neapolitan . . ."

Joe, the bearded one, appeared first; Henry, the black one, was behind him, holding out a gun. Parini appeared, with his third hired hand in front of him.

Three guns under the taxi-driver's nose. I watch the whole scene like a spectator. Almost half-heartedly. And already resigned.

"The guy is mine . . . dickhead," Parini grunts at the Neapolitan. "*Non c'è problèma . . . Non c'è problèma! Calma!*"

No time to say a word. Henry and Joe picked me up like a sack of manure, and threw me into the back of their car. Parini's set off first, towards Sora, and Henry followed while Joe held my head down below the seat with the gun at my temple.

While my forehead rubbed against the leather of the seat, they carried on talking in their impenetrable New York slang. I tried to understand the odd word, to get an idea of the fate they had in store for me. One said he felt like mortadella. He was amazed that you could get pizza in Italy too, only not so good as at home. The other said that the rental cars in Rome were real old bangers. But I'm not sure I'd quite understood everything.

* * *

"Have you thought about it, Polsinelli?"

With my face just a few inches from the sludge, I bellowed yes straight away. The banks of the Liri were absolutely deserted. Henry and Joe, who'd been holding me out above the river by my hair, brought me back to the bank.

"Twenty-five per cent?"

"It's okay."

"It's okay? Well, where've you put it then?" asked Parini as he tucked into a huge dripping slice of cold pizza.

"What do you mean?"

When he clicked his fingers I was treated to the little freshening up exercise that I thought I'd managed to avoid.

The cloudy water went up my nose and chilled my eyes. I hung on for a few seconds without moving, then I shook my head frantically to get them to cut short their torture. It seemed to go on for a century. I even felt like diving right in but I couldn't shake off the hand clamped over my neck.

"All I can see is that you tried to give us the slip, but maybe I'm wrong? Where have you put it?" Parini asked as I filled my lungs again.

"I haven't . . . got . . . the money on me."

Parini threw his pizza crust into the water and wiped his fingers on a handkerchief one of the others had handed to him.

"Listen, Polsinelli. I was born here but I'm not planning on ending up here. But if you would like to, we could arrange it. I'm not going to hang around with these arseholes. The place we stayed in last night was enough, my guys thought they were sleeping in a cowshed. So, *basta*, d'you get it?"

"I don't have the dosh. . . Wait till the next harvest."

He clicked his fingers. I screamed in fear and they ducked me under right up to my waist. My mouth filled with water and I thought my lungs would burst.

My body stopped struggling instantly.

Dead time.

They dragged me onto the bank.

A slap revived me.

"Now it's fifty-fifty, Polsinelli. *Meta per uno, capish?* Fifty-fifty, okay?"

"...Yes..."

"You're in debt, Polsinelli. Tomorrow I want to see you with half of what you got from selling the 30,000 litres. Got that?"

No, I hadn't got it at all. I heard the car doors slamming in the distance. My face was hidden in wet, muddy, tall grass. My breathing settled gradually. I closed my eyes. My wet clothes chilled me to the bone but I didn't have the strength to take them off. A car sped past but no one saw me. I wanted to drag myself to the side of the road to stop someone. And go home to Bianca. Not that I knew whether she would still have me. But I gave up on that too. I regained consciousness just enough to avoid asking for help from some guy who couldn't have wished for anything more than to run me over ... and more than once, just to be sure.

You're having your revenge, Sant'Angelo ...

That's the only explanation. Do you really bear me that much of a grudge?

Ask whatever you like of me. Make me atone for what I have done. But a little mercy, please.

Do something.

Just a sign.

I crawled along the ground until I found a flat dry rock, and I laid my head on it.

* * *

Night.

A car door slamming. I thought it was them coming back.

Two men dressed all in black bent over me and heaved me out of the ditch, one carrying me by the

156

armpits and the other by my legs. And they put me in the back of a Mercedes. It was as they put a blanket over my shoulders that I recognized the two emissaries from the Vatican.

Sitting right next to me, I finally got to see the face of the man who'd accompanied the bishop the day before but hadn't got out of the car.

A thin face, little oval glasses, close-cropped hair, thick lips displaying a calm smile. He's wearing a black suit with a little cross on his lapel. He's waited patiently for me to gather my wits, not moving, not saying a word. I've wrapped myself in the blanket, curling myself up as tightly as possible.

"This is a trying time for you . . ."

"You speak French?"

"I speak four languages, but I don't use yours as often as I would like to."

"You're doing pretty well."

A serene voice which appeases everything around it. A completely relaxed expression, eyes that look dead ahead and never blink. No comparison with all those hysterical individuals who are all teeth and who spit out every sentence. He lays the tips of his fingers on my arm.

"Don't catch cold. It's very dangerous in summer."

"Are you taking me back?"

"Of course."

He gestures to his men to get back in the car and set off. I don't have to give them the address.

"Who can claim to understand our Lord's mysterious ways? Do you own this vineyard, Signor Polsinelli?"

"Yes. And you are . . .?"

"My name won't mean much to you. Let's say I'm a man of finance – someone has to be, don't they? It's actually quite a demanding task, managing Church property and funds."

157

My eyes question him silently.

"I won't go into detail, but for simplicity's sake you could say that I was rather like the banker . . . Yes, let's call me the Vatican's banker."

A light bulb goes on in my head. The Vatican cellars, the Vatican treasures and all the stories you hear about them. I start to shake but I am no longer sure it is because of the cold. I manage to control a flood of curiosity which would lead to hundreds of questions, each more indiscreet than the last.

"Tomorrow we're going to hold this mass. You've probably guessed that a ceremony like that acts as an 'officialization' – is that the right word? – by the Church. Do you realize what that implies?"

That the miracle has been sanctioned. The vineyard officially becomes an authentic sacred site. Recognized and honoured by the highest authority.

That's going too far for me. I didn't want things to get this far. Neither did Dario. Now I can understand why the two men making the enquiries were so thorough.

"Thousands of pilgrims will come to pray at the feet of Sant'Angelo. A new chapel will have to be built, services arranged etc . . . Tomorrow will be a big day. What do you think of all this?"

That it's all wrong. I hadn't predicted any of this. None of it. Not the tidal wave of business propositions, not the Americans pitching up, not the greed of the local community, nor the finger of God pointing to his sacrament. I just wanted a lucky break, a miracle landing in my lap, and, *basta*, I would set off home with my takings. That's all.

He crosses his arms, still with the same strange smile on his lips. When I think about it, I wonder whether it really is a smile.

"But just imagine for a moment that instead of granting this blessing we announce to the faithful that this whole diabolical exercise has only been set up to extract money. That godless sinners have violated the memory of Sant'Angelo to line their own pockets . . ."

"What exactly are you saying . . . I don't . . ."

"That the chapel burned with the help of petrol, that the statue had been fire-proofed, that the building was carefully 'prepared' so that it opened up like that, and that Marcello Di Palma is a remarkable actor. Do you deny it?"

Deny it?

What would be the point. Right from the start I had the feeling that the guys were not the sort to go singing hosannas in front of a few dead embers. Dario tried to play a game of wits with the ministers from on high. There it is. And, like an idiot, I followed it through. What made me think I'd be clever enough to pit myself against them?

So then, Antonio, how do you look now? It had to end sooner or later. Next to these guys, Parini and his three little sidekicks look like clowns.

"What are you planning to do?" I ask.

"Publicly announce the sacrilege. Hand you over to the authorities, and mother Church will see to it that you don't get out of prison for thirty years. It has the power to do that. Just imagine the disappointment for the faithful and everyone you've deceived. The people of Sora, and the rest of the region. And that's only how you'll be judged on this earth. Far less terrifying. You have committed the ultimate sin."

Far less terrifying? Perhaps, but, given the choice, I'd rather precipitate my final judgement than end my days in prison.

"Unless . . ."

I sit up with a jolt to grasp this tantalizing phrase. All the cogs in my mind swing into motion. The car is already in the town.

"Unless you and I find some sort of *modus vivendi.* The best solution for everyone. The most important thing is to spare the faithful from such a cruel admission. As I've already said, who can claim to understand the Lord's mysterious ways? Perhaps he chose you specially to pay homage to the good Sant'Angelo who was so quickly forgotten, I will grant you that . . ."

Silence. I'm biting my lip to stop myself saying anything stupid.

"And we would know what to do with all the money that this wine could bring in. We have a great many projects. Building hospitals, creating a sacred site, schools . . . We haven't yet decided. We need so much money for all the good works that remain to be done. This wine could be a gift for so many unlucky people. I have to tell you, but we were amazed by just how many parishes wanted to use Sant'Angelo's wine to celebrate mass. That's when we thought that we could make it the official communion wine all over Italy . . ."

"You are joking?"

"Do I look as if I am, Signor Polsinelli? But none of this is actually anything to do with you. What I'm proposing is very simple: you give everything over, the deeds of the property, the stock of wine, and all your pitiful calculations. We know how to proceed far better than any of the little administrators you've been seeing. In other words, make us a gift . . ."

"A gift?"

"Well, that's how it would look to everyone. In

160

return, every year we would put 500,000 of your francs into an anonymous account which you would have opened at a bank of your choice."

The car stops outside Bianca's house. The last customers at the bar are completely mesmerized to see me arriving in a Mercedes. The driver gets out to open the door for me. The barman thinks he must be hallucinating.

"I've heard that you're having trouble with the locals. And with other people, too, perhaps . . ."

"You're very well informed."

"The ways of the Lord are impenetrable, are they not . . .? Think about my proposal. But are you in any position to refuse?"

No. Of course not. He knows that as well as I do.

"And be assured that, should you accept our offer, you will benefit from our complete protection. I don't think anyone would dare put it to the test."

Before leaving he adds: "Please don't worry about that. Shall I come and pick you up at about 11 o'clock? We could go to the ceremony together, couldn't we?"

He winds the window back up and the car slips away in silence.

All around me I can see silent, astonished faces full of loathing.

But no one dares come right up to me.

It is as if there is a magnetic field with a thirty-foot radius around me.

Bianca has seen everything from her window. She disappears for a moment.

And I hear the front door opening.

*   *   *

161

"I tell you we forgot to bolt it."

"It's bolted and double locked, I've already checked, Antonio. You should be trying to sleep, it's almost dawn."

"But why would I want to sleep? Have you got any sleeping pills? What's the time . . . or some Valium, yes, that's good stuff . . . Or Temazepam, just a couple. Please."

"I haven't got anything like that . . . I could make you some herbal tea . . ."

"Herbal tea! Who are you trying to kid? These shutters are useless . . . they don't do anything, look . . . Have you got anything to drink? Some grappa, anything . . . I don't know."

"Some wine?"

"Some wine . . . I don't want to hear anything more about bloody wine. I want . . . I want to . . . How do you say 'throw up' in your language? Throw up, don't you wops ever throw up? I'm sure the door's not bolted, sometimes you can be sure you've done something, really convinced, so much so that you forget to do it. What's the time . . . ?"

* * *

"Wake up, Antonio. It's nearly time for the mass."

. . . The vineyard . . . I must get to the vineyard . . .

"Bianca? What time is it?"

"Nearly eleven. You only got to sleep a couple of hours ago."

Yes . . . I remember. The sun's already high in the sky. My eyelids won't open . . . I must get to the vineyard . . . the banker's right. Without his protection I've had it. He'll handle everything. And I can go back to Paris . . .

162

"Is there a car waiting for me downstairs?"

"Yes. A big one."

I sense a sort of uneasiness in her voice when she says that, and my eyes open of their own accord.

"A Mercedes?"

"No. A Cadillac."

I gaze at her fearfully.

"And the second one's trying to park . . ."

I throw myself at Bianca and shake her violently, shouting, "Are you going to let me die here, or something!"

"You're going mad, Antonio!" she cries and bursts into tears as she slaps me full in the face.

I glance outside through the curtains. There they are. Waiting for me. The Mercedes is nowhere to be seen.

"Help me, Bianca . . ."

She wipes her tears with the corner of her apron. Slowly she gets her breath back and she thinks for a moment.

"Do you really want to get out?"

"Yes . . ."

"My father's Vespa is down on the patio. It still works, I lend it to people quite often."

"And?"

"I'll go down first to keep them busy for a minute while you slip away. Then all I can do is pray for you, Antonio . . ."

* * *

Five minutes later we're down by the side door. The machine starts first time.

"What are you going to tell them? These guys aren't like the ones on TV."

I sit astride the scooter and she goes out. I wait for a moment and hurtle off down the street without looking back. A car only just misses me, I make the engine scream.

I speed down the Via Nazionale with three turns of the accelerator, I can't look behind me any more, people are yelling as I pass them, the sun's blinding.

Don't look back . . .

The road gets narrower, I'm already on the outskirts of the town.

I leave the tarmac and set off on the stony track.

There are a few sheep up ahead of me, and the shepherd raises his arms to warn me. I slow down for a moment and glance behind me. The Cadillacs are on my heels, I swerve round the sheep too quickly and skid into the ditch, screaming.

Thrown into a tree.

In a daze I manage to get to my feet, bent double and with one of my ankles making me scream with pain. The shepherd's lunging towards me, shouting and brandishing his stick. I head off into the woods. Two shots ring out, I run on aimlessly, whipped by branches and tripping on the undergrowth. The burning in my ankle forces hoarse cries of pain from me, cries I try to stifle, for fear that they'll betray my position.

The bastards are going to get me . . .

It's a huge forest. If I can lose myself in it the others might get lost too . . . I don't know how to get to the vineyard . . . I'm going to have to stop for a minute to get my bearings in this jungle . . .

Impossible. There isn't time.

The bastards won't get me.

*   *   *

164

I ran for a long time with my ankle burning, although I didn't actually feel the pain. I collapsed to the ground, completely out of breath.

Everything went quiet again.

And I waited. Panting like a flayed bull.

I slowly lifted my head. And, in the distance, through the foliage, I saw this window.

A sentence came back to me.

Can you see the lights over there behind the trees? That's where I live. I just wanted to let you know . . . if you want somewhere to hide . . .

It's Mangini's house. Without yet knowing why, I heaved a sigh.

* * *

Tears came to my eyes when he opened the door. We stood there in front of each other for a moment, not knowing what to say.

"Signor Polsinelli?"

He showed me into a big, almost bare room with a huge oak table nearly ten feet long. I sit down and rub my ankle, drunk with exhaustion. Mangini behaves with cool detachment, as if he hasn't sensed that I'm frightened for my life.

"I must have invited sir here ten times since he arrived, but I didn't think he would come today . . . not today when everyone's buzzing round his plot of land."

"Buzzing a bit too much. They all want . . ."

I shut my trap just in time, on the brink of confiding in him.

"Tell me, Signor Mangini, could I rest for a while here? People are looking for me, it would take too long to explain . . ."

He heads over to a cupboard and takes out his rifle, then loads it and lays it down on the table.

"No one will find you here. Unless sir told someone that he was going over to see that old brigand Mangini?"

"No, no one knows."

Within his walls, in his presence, with his rifle. I suddenly feel safe.

"Actually . . . you're not all that old, Signor Mangini."

"Can sir guess my age?"

"Sixty."

"Thank you. I'll be seventy-three next month. What does sir think of my house?" he adds, and it's only then that I notice his courteous third-person has come back like an automatic reflex.

It's beautiful. A little three-storey villa right in the heart of the forest. A perfect refuge for a hermit who doesn't look his age.

"I built it myself in '53. All by myself. Not one man from the village came and helped me," he said with a mixture of rancour and pride, with a nasty, vengeful note I wouldn't have expected. Then he adds: "Because everyone in this village hates me, didn't anyone tell sir?"

I don't understand why he says that but, given what the people of Sora have put me through, I'm prepared to believe him.

"Everyone seems to respect you, Signor Mangini."

"It's not respect, it's just silence!"

I don't make any attempt to delve deeper. All I want is to stay as long as I can in this house which smells of good dry stone and waxed wood.

In fact, as we are talking, a smell creeps up on me almost by surprise, swelling gradually while I look all round the room trying to work out where it is coming

166

from. Mangini doesn't seem to notice it, as if his nose has been saturated with it for years. Mine quivers a few times, gradually growing accustomed to the smell, and I've already almost forgotten it's there. A strange smell, a mixture, with a vegetable quality, hot and bland at the same time, colourless. It doesn't remind me of anything I already know, but suggests a mixture of things which, taken independently, have always been part of my life.

"Come on, sir needs to get some rest, he can take off his jacket, Signor Polsinelli. He must be hungry with everything that's going on, isn't he? I was just about to eat, actually. Can he smell something good on the way, from behind there?"

Food? A smell of nosh? I would have thought of everything except that, the scent of dried hay, the mustiness of a book of pressed plants that hasn't been opened for years, a waft from embers or ashes, anything except something that was being cooked with a view to being eaten. This is very unlike Bianca's house, where the least little whiff makes me feel like having an entire Roman banquet. And yet there's nothing really repugnant about whatever it is simmering away. Strange, yes, but nothing more.

He laid the table in two swift movements. When he took out a third plate I got up slowly.

"Were you expecting someone?"

"Yes. A relation. Sir must sit back down."

"Listen, I'm not very hungry, you weren't expecting me and I don't want to be any trouble . . ."

Mangini takes out a bottle and fills two glasses with wine.

"It's my nephew, my sister's son. He comes to see me every now and then. We've become close since his mother died. And if it weren't for him I honestly think

167

I wouldn't talk to anyone from one year to the next. But if you don't want to stay my nephew can take you back to Sora as soon as he gets here. How would that be?"

"No, not to Sora, to the vineyard. I have to go to my vineyard."

"For the mass? As sir wishes! . . . So? Are you staying?"

Of course I am. I can't do anything else. I don't want to any more. I glance quickly at the rifle. He notices.

"You've nothing to be afraid of now, no one will find you here. Sit down in the sitting room until my nephew gets here, and while I just put the water on to boil."

My ankle hurts less, it's not a fracture or even a sprain. Just for a change of scene I walk out of the dining room, past the kitchen from which the indescribable smell is emanating, and into a large room dominated by a tattered old armchair in front of a big trunk which must act as a foot-stool. Exactly what I need. There is absolutely nothing else around it. Icy emptiness. No TV, no framed family photographs, no magazines. Just an armchair and a trunk. Deliberately sparse. Peculiar.

What time would you spend in a room like that? What would you go there for? To rest, to forget?

Or quite the opposite. Would you gather your thoughts there, the fruits of your meditations and memories? You'd have to have everything in your head already.

"Has sir found something to ease the waiting, Signor Polsinelli?" he calls from the depths of the kitchen.

Found what? There's nothing to find here; you might just be able to lose whatever you had when you came in. This room must be for waiting for things to come up of their own accord. You just have to wait. And slowly, slowly, they fall into place. They emerge.

The trunk is right at my feet. Tempting.

I look over towards the kitchen, put one hand on the catch. Without making a sound, I lift the lid.

I had to lift it all the way up in order to make out the only two things inside it. First I blinked, then I screwed up my eyes.

To try to believe them . . .

At the bottom of the wooden chasm I saw this great thick pile of folded black fabric with its black collar impeccably smooth and rigid. Next to it there was a pistol which looked like a Luger. The pistol should have terrified me. But it was more the shirt that gave me a shock. The black shirt with the red initial on the collar. An M.

I can feel my heart pounding in my temples.

They were always good and clean those bastards, but towards the end they weren't so proud any more, the fascists. I don't know why, but the compare *and me, we were terrified of the concentration camps. There wasn't really any reason to be, but we were still frightened we'd be sent to our deaths. That's how it was, that's why we tried not to come across any of them. But it happened, from time to time, and they'd taunt us and call us cowards. I didn't dare raise my voice, which proves that they must have been right. But I wanted to tell them that my only honour, in all this mess which had got us that far, was that I hadn't met a single person who wanted to kill me, that I hadn't met a single person I wanted to kill, that I'd never seen the front line in my life, and during their pig's ear of a campaign in Greece I just waited for it to blow over of its own accord. For four long years. And it wasn't over yet.*

"It's nearly ready, Signor Polsinelli!"

A former fascist . . .

Mangini was in Mussolini's troops. One of those fanatics my father kept bumping into, right to the end. I didn't know there were any of them left, real ones,

169

like the ones you see in the films, so clean and black, companions in death blinded by the impeccable, silky-smooth Duce. The Mussolini M on the shirt was reserved for officers. A privilege. My host wasn't just anybody.

"I hope sir's hungry!"

Hungry . . .? A real fascist asking me to dinner, taking me in, protecting me. Worrying whether or not I'm hungry. I closed the trunk.

He makes sweeping gestures to get me to sit at the table. The way he holds his head, his violence, his natural reserve, his reclusiveness . . . all these details muddled up together. And they can all be explained and, even if I'm wrong, I can't help myself dressing them all up in a black shirt.

"It's almost ready, sit yourself down, my stupid nephew has only got a minute to get here while the pasta's still hot. You're going to taste my speciality. *Ammazza!*"

I don't know what to do any more, leave, spit in his face, scream at him all the things my father would want to say. If he hasn't burned his shirt and thrown his pistol on the fire, that must be a sign of nostalgia. To each his war. To each his memories. To each his trophies.

I thought I'd made a friend.

But despite all the disgust he inspires in me, I would have to be mad to insult him and leave the place when there are guys who want to kill me out there. I'm cornered. And forced to choose the lesser of two evils.

"I hardly boil it at all, that's how it should be eaten. Do you know why the Italians eat their pasta al dente? Because it's poor man's food, and when times were hard they ate it almost raw so that it carried on swelling in the stomach, it stays in your tummy much longer like that."

170

"Can you smell that fetid smell?" I ask.

"What smell . . .?"

"That smell of cooking."

"My sauce?"

"Is it made with castor oil?"

He crosses his arms and looks at me in astonishment, then his quiet little smile reappears.

"You don't cook with castor oil."

"Of course, I was forgetting, quite the opposite, you purge with it."

Silence. I still haven't sat down. He goes back to his kitchen without picking up on my reference to the purges. I already regret it, it almost fell out. As if I desperately wanted him to chuck me out of his house. His voice just carries to me over the sound of frying.

"He's young, Signor Polsinelli . . . but I still admire him. He talks like one of the boys from round here, he's like the boys from round here, he looks after himself as well as the boys from round here. You could be forgiven for thinking all our local boys are now born in Vitry-sur-Seine."

I stay standing for a moment, unable to make a decision, not knowing what to say.

"Let's eat!"

Everything seems confused. Him, his age, his past, what he's lived through and all the things I don't want to know about. He comes back from the kitchen carrying a big bowl up in the air as if it were a chalice. The strange smell wafts over from the bowl, and when he puts it under my nose I have to put my hand to my mouth to stifle the urge to retch.

"It's perfect . . . perfect! If sir doesn't like this, I could quickly make something else, but it would be a shame."

His enthusiasm seems increasingly sincere. He smiles and pats my shoulder. I feel as though he wants me to share in his eager appetite.

I gulp back my disgust and look at the plate he's serving out for me. A whitish magma without any sauce, not even a drop of oil, little threads of green, boiled leaves here and there, and a sort of yellow emulsion which does nothing to cheer the whole thing up. Nothing aesthetically pleasing about it, so bound to be nothing pleasing about the taste. Only the bland smell has become hotter and more violent.

He sits down happily and gives me his kindest smile. We descend into silence.

I slowly take my hand away from my mouth. Close my eyes. And it is only now that the crucial point becomes clear.

I suppress another retch, I'm sweating, I won't be able to control my stomach much longer.

"What's going on, Antonio? Doesn't sir like rigatoni?"

Looking at it again, I can see it all, the maize kernels, the dandelions, the pungent smell of mint . . .

It's a haunting, obsessive smell. It goes to my head.

How could you have eaten this, Dario?

I lean to one side, a more powerful retch forces my mouth open, and I spew a little thread of bile which burns my throat.

Mangini gets to his feet, disconcerted, and spreads his hands to show his embarrassment.

Do you understand now, Antoine? Did you feel safe in this house? And now you'd give anything to be back outside? But, you see, you might still have a chance of getting out . . . because Mangini still hasn't realized that you've got it . . . got the fact that he's the one who killed Dario.

"I have to say I've had more appreciative guests, Antonio Polsinelli . . . you're going to offend me."

"I'm so sorry, it'll pass . . ."

"My apologies, I'm very fond of this recipe. I could put together any sauce in Italy, even the most amazing ones, but I don't like cooking things that you could find in the first restaurant you set foot in. With cooking you have to dare to be different!"

"Excuse me, Signor Mangini . . . I'm not feeling well . . . I'm all hot and cold . . . I'll just get some fresh air outside, then I'll feel better."

As soon as I get to my feet, he puts his hand on the rifle. I understand, and so does he. I slump back against the door without taking my eyes off the old madman, I try to find the handle and the door opens all by itself . . .

I cried out loud when someone grabbed my hair from behind.

And again when they punched me in the back. And my face crashed down on a piece of furniture. I had to hold my ribs as I coughed. I wanted to get back up but a kick in the face forced me to stay down.

I don't know how long that interlude lasted, but I drew it out as long as possible to avoid more blows.

Mangini leant over me and I curled up a little more tightly.

"Could sir stand up so that I can introduce my nephew, whom he already knows."

Porteglia leant forward, rubbing his fist, as if preparing to hit me again. The first time I was blind drunk, the second I had my back to him. Which probably means you shouldn't be afraid of a little shit like him.

"*Sole il nipote capisce lo zio,*" Mangini told me.

"Only the nephew can understand the uncle." It

sounds like a dictum. You have to mull it over to get the meaning of it, if there is one, and right now I can't see it. "The uncle and the nephew": it sounds like an Italian farce. One of them's nearly a father and the other's a false son. Tied by blood but with no respect for their roles. Complicity without obligation. Playing the game rather than doing anything serious. You just had to look at how they'd gone about this, taking it in turns to toy with me, as thick as two thieves in a fable ... and I'm the unfortunate victim. A fable, that's it. With no obvious moral.

"Come on, sir must do honour to my speciality. He must make a bit of an effort!"

To underline his invitation he shows me the pistol which he's taken out of the trunk and is loading ostentatiously. As if the rifle on its own wasn't enough. Porteglia grabs hold of me, lifts me up and pushes me onto a chair. They probably think I'll eat with a gun to my head. Specially this dead man's dish. Eating that is like preparing to pass over to the other side. The nephew sits down on my left, and the uncle puts a fork in my hand, as you would for a child, then he leans close to my ear as any mother would to get her little one to eat. "What's the matter with sir? ... Mmm? Has Attilio made you lose your appetite? Or was it the shirt sir saw in my trunk? Has he never seen one before? And does he really think he would have found it if I hadn't wanted him to see it? Is he afraid of the dark, something that dark?"

I tried for a long time to find something to say in reply, but I could only come up with insults. And in French. Insults are the most instinctive aspect of language.

"Fascist pig."

"Anyone would think I speak French, I understood

174

that perfectly . . . But I'm used to it, with the locals. And they're wrong too. I wasn't a real fascist. Not for long, anyway. I may have kept the shirt, but not as a relic. It's more like a shroud, a ghost's shroud which I keep carefully locked away in that trunk."

"Fascist pig."

Porteglia belted me across the back of the neck. That was when I leapt at him to try to drive my fork into his eye. Just like that. From the cry he let out I really thought I'd succeeded, but all I actually did was rip his cheek open.

Obviously he hammered me with blows again, down on the ground, even breaking a cheekbone with the toe of his shoe. He was trying to blind me, and was about to do so when the uncle pushed him aside.

"Dario didn't make such a fuss," the uncle tells me.

The nephew sits back down with one hand covering half his face. The injury's given him an incredible surge of energy. I get back up, holding one hand over my eye.

"Quite the opposite! He really liked old Uncle Mangini's cooking, didn't he now? I seem to remember finding a bottle of Gevrey-Chambertin '76 in a little shop near the Palais-Royal, to go with the rigatoni. Wonderful, wasn't it, my dear uncle?"

No reply.

"That's where I went to study wine, and I've still got my little studio on the Rue de la Banque, that's where we invited Dario to come for some supper. God, I love Paris."

"It was the first time I'd been, and I won't set foot in the place again," said Mangini, keeping one hand on his gun. "I'd even forgotten how to fire this thing. . . if you think about it, the war was fifty years ago . . . and even then I didn't use it much. I wasn't much of a soldier . . ."

I closed my eyes.

"But that cunning little Dario, it was exactly what he deserved. Six months earlier he came and bought the land off me, and it made me laugh at the time . . . It was only afterwards, when I saw him hanging round the chapel instead of destroying it, and asking questions about Sant'Angelo, that I started to see what he had in mind. I even remember one day stupidly saying to him that if he managed to make good wine from the place, then that would be a real miracle, and that made him laugh!"

Porteglia spears a piece of pasta with his fork and puts it under my nose. I don't open my mouth. He rubs it against my lips and Mangini aims his pistol at me. I part my lips slightly.

"At first I thought he must be mad, but then . . . Sir should put himself in my shoes, Signor Polsinelli, I was practically born there, on that plot of land, and I never saw a thing . . . It took a stupid little idiot from Paris who was still wet behind the ears to have this wild idea . . . I lost a lot of sleep over that."

I chew it without breathing, it doesn't taste of anything, not even salt. I close my eyes very tightly. And spit the whole lot back onto the table.

"So I told him that I knew exactly what he was up to, that I really liked his idea and that he wouldn't be able to do it without me. I gave him time to think about it and then I went to Paris for just one evening, time enough for the three of us to have supper together and talk. He offered me ten per cent of the action, pitiful, not enough to buy myself a cup of coffee . . . And I killed him, because what was supposed to happen was that the land would go to his mother, and I would just

176

buy the whole lot off her, perfectly simple, and I'd be the one to bring Sant'Angelo back all on my own."

I still haven't opened my eyes and I'm forcing myself not to listen to any more. The only thing that matters is the torture with the fork.

From the winter of '44 onwards we started eating whatever we could lay our hands on. I even remember one wood where we managed to last several days on just redcurrants. Another time I found a whole load of tortoises, dozens of them, God knows why, but nothing could surprise me any more in that place. You had to accept whatever came your way. It took a pick-axe to break the shells. And you needed fourteen tortoises to get a decent helping of meat. The best thing was eggs. The compare *used to make a pretty good ragout with them. He could put together dishes made up of all sorts of crap from around and about, as well as anything we could risk our lives to steal from local farmers. With these crusts, and dandelions and bits and bobs of things, he managed to feed us – we never asked exactly what it was, the important thing was that he managed, so much so in fact that the five of us that were there at the time ended up thinking he was the best chef in the world. We were never sick once, you know . . . Well, granted, most of the time we had to think about something else when we were actually putting the food in our mouths, but he was a magician all the same. He really had a talent for it, it was the only thing he could do to make me happy and to pay me back for all the times I'd saved his life.*

"Then the solicitor told me that a new *padrone* was on his way. I gnawed my fingers to the bone, then. That's understandable, isn't it? Almost the same as Dario, but with something missing, or something extra, I don't really know. And it was simple, I told myself all was not lost and that I could still buy the land off him before he grasped what was going on . . . But not even money, not even beatings . . . there was

177

nothing for it, the new boy from Paris was even more tenacious than the first."

. . . Christmas '44, I can't say we had much faith left in God. We were all thinking of someone. A fiancée, a child, and we would all have liked to be able to tell that person that we had defended them or protected them. Protected them, my arse . . . Four years later and we had even less idea what the hell we were doing there, at Christmas time. And really nothing left to eat this time. We didn't believe in God anymore, or he was the only thing left we did believe in because that particular 25th of December, you'll have to take my word for this, we experienced what you might call a miracle. Yes, a miracle, I can't think of another word for it. We'd heard that a fascist garrison had been set up four miles from our little hole, complete with fresh supplies. We wondered which one of us should go: two of us were dying of cold, little Roberto was terrified, and you couldn't say the compare *was a shining example of courage. Anyway, it just had to be me because I couldn't hold out there any longer, I wanted to go . . . The* compare *tried to stop me going, he was frightened of dying without me by his side, and I promised I would come back. Robertino gave me his shoes and I set off. And I did come back. And I can't even tell you what happened because I don't really remember very much. I talked to them, I pretended to say things and to listen to them, to ask them for news of Italy, but I didn't give a damn about any of that, all I could think of was the food stores. I ate and they made fun of me, one of the officers told me I could join his detachment, all I had to do was put the uniform on if I wanted a chance of getting back home. I played the fool, I said that could wait till the end of the night. They all went off to bed and I stole eighteen pounds of pasta from them. Eighteen! That tells you something . . . Eighteen . . . I put the whole lot in a canteen, I thought I was going to die I was so tired, but I don't know why, just the thought that I was going to get away from them gave me new*

strength, and I went back to the others who were still waiting for me. We all cried like babies when I showed them the treasure. Yellow like gold . . . I can't tell you now what that felt like . . . I'd stolen pasta without even knowing what sort it was, it was the dead of night . . . and in the first light of dawn I realized that we had before us something that would see us through the days to come, eighteen pounds of rigatoni . . .

A slap from Porteglia brings me back to the present. They've finished their food. Mangini's picking his teeth, very relaxed, almost slumped in his chair. Porteglia's pouring himself another glass of wine and he smacks his lips with satisfaction as he tastes it.

"What a beautiful miracle he laid on for us, our Signor Polsinelli . . . It was a good idea doing it on the day of the Gonfalone . . . but there's one thing I can't understand and that's Marcello . . ."

They both freeze at the same time, exchanging a look, then they come over to me.

"Are you going to tell us, then?" says the nephew.

"Of course he's going to tell us what happened with that blind bastard. I've known the old drunk for years. I've only ever known him crawling along the ground and begging, so you can't take me for a bloody fool with this story of a miracle . . ."

. . . A miracle, at Christmas, I mean if you're going to have one it might as well be then . . . When you haven't eaten pasta for months and months – longer even – it's better than a miracle. The compare *promised us he wouldn't ruin it for us, and because it was a special day he would do his very best, so he gathered up the best he could find. He invented a recipe on the spot. Some maize stolen from a barn, some mint, and dandelions. What would have really made it would have been to have had some red, some tomatoes, but even God couldn't manage that where we were, so the* compare *invented*

179

Rigatoni all'albanese . . . *We cut up the wood we had left to build a big fire for the cooking pot and we sat ourselves round it as if we were at the cinema, and the smell of the sauce gradually got to us, and I've never smelt anything like it in all my life, my stomach opened up like a chasm, and I felt as if I could eat the whole eighteen pounds . . .*

This time Porteglia punches me in the nose, something snaps inside and it starts oozing blood.

The bit about the blind man really annoys them. It's the only part of the whole set up they can't work out, and Mangini and his nephew won't kill me until they know. There's blood running down over my lips, and I don't know . . . I don't know . . .

All of a sudden my eyes fill with tears.

After our feast we lay there for an hour without saying a word, with our bellies in the air, waiting for our whole bodies to feel the pleasure, undisturbed. D'you know, now that we'd got over our hunger we were all thinking about the same thing . . . wine . . . wine . . . red wine . . . But even God couldn't come up with that where we were . . . And asking for two miracles in the same day . . . Robertino, who was a good little Catholic, told us about the multiplication of the bread and the wine, and we asked him to go back over the bit about the wine. One of us swore that if he ever got home he would become a wine producer and he would never sell any to anyone, but he didn't get home. The eighteen pounds of rigatoni gave us more time to play with, we made it last and last, and the compare *got used to making his sauce, we couldn't get him to try anything new . . . In spite of everything, we were just waiting to die, expecting to. Like all soldiers, we thought about it. Except that we weren't even soldiers any more . . . I can tell you, I've already paid my dues, my son, for you and your brother, and for any sons you might have, and you'd better never find yourselves in a shit-hole like that . . .*

Mangini can't stand it any longer. My silence has

aggravated his resentment. Why would he want to let me live?

"You'll never get the benefit of all this money, Antonio . . . I'd be too ashamed. It would be too painful for me. And how could I let you leave this place, hmm? Now that you know I killed the other little arsehole."

I try my best to talk.

To negotiate.

To struggle.

But I can't even open my mouth any more.

I'm going to meet the same end as you, Dario.

I really should be feeling frightened.

But it won't come.

I don't know why.

"Shame . . . I would really like to have understood Dario's last trick . . . How he gave that shit of a blind man his sight back . . . Because that was one of Dario's ideas, wasn't it? You really were very alike, you two . . ."

Mangini grabs my chin between his thumb and forefinger, squeezing hard and turning my face so that he can get an even closer look at it. His voice is gentler now. I see a brief glimmer of kindness in his eyes.

"You, Antonio . . . you're a bit like Dario . . . But there's someone else you're even more like . . . much more . . . hardly surprising, really . . ."

In February Robertino died on the road to Tirana, and it was down to just the compare *and me, like it had been from the start. It was a bit of a mystery, it was like we were immortal so long as we stayed together, and in mortal danger if we got a bit too far apart. We trudged on, thinking about the boat. Then one night we saw an encampment with fire and noise, and the* compare *was all spent, he wanted to go over straight away. And I stopped him, you see we didn't know what we might find, Germans, the Albanian resistance, fascists, friends or enemies, we were better off waiting till*

181

morning. And as we went to sleep I told him: "Trust me, you idiot, it hasn't done you any harm this far." . . . Well, would you believe, the next morning I was woken by someone kicking me . . . Fascists, I'd hit the jackpot, and I thought the com- pare *and me were even deeper in the shit than we had been, and I looked up and I saw the stupid bastard standing over me, all clean, all in black. At first I didn't really get it, I wasn't properly awake, I remember looking at him and saying: "Hey, come on . . . Have you gone mad, or what? We've got to get home, we can't just fuck around here." I don't know what he'd gone and told them but one of them took out a revolver and asked me to follow him. I ran like a madman and that's when I got this bullet in the leg. The pain still runs through me to this day. They must have thought I was dead, and no one came to check . . . not even him . . .*

I'm not frightened. Mangini's still cradling my head in his hand. He picks up his gun and points it at my temple.

"Why did you get mixed up in all this, Polsinelli? When I heard your name it took me right back in time . . . a long way back . . . I've only ever known one Polsinelli . . ."

He's watching even more intently, I can't stand it, I close my eyes again.

"The devil must have done this on purpose, playing this trick of fate on me . . . nearly fifty years later . . . So I waited for you and I laughed."

His hand has started shaking, my eyes are screwed tight shut.

After the explosion I fell to the floor, I screamed and I saw . . .

The broken window.

Porteglia sprawled on the floor and Mangini, stand- ing motionless, holding his right side with both his hands.

182

Outside, beyond the window, a silhouette.

I haven't been touched.

Porteglia bellows, the door opens. I'm alive. Mangini staggers for a moment, then leans on the table till his forehead comes to rest on it. I never thought I was going to die.

Someone comes in. Mangini looks up. I'm fine. Everything's okay.

My father. In the doorway.

There he is.

Porteglia drags himself over to me, begging me.

I was never afraid.

I recognized his halting step. He goes over towards Mangini, recharges his rifle and rams the barrel into his neck.

And I kept thinking of the compare *and wondering what had come over him. We always managed without anyone else, without the army, without an officer, without weapons, without food, all we had keeping us warm was that urge to get home, and so long as we were together we missed the worst of it, and we'd rather have gone naked than have worn a black shirt, or a red one or a khaki one. And, d'you know, I felt sorry for him . . . To have scraped past so much shit and then to fall right into it just when the end was in sight . . . I really didn't know how he was going to live with it when he got back home. All I felt for him was pity . . .*

He didn't try to meet my eye. He was only interested in Mangini, splayed across the table. They said a few things to each other, with their eyes, things that had nothing to do with me, and took quite a time.

Two old men.

Far away.

More than forty-five years ago now.

They had plenty to say, just by looking.

At each other.

"Shall we go home?"

It could have sounded like a question, but it was very much a suggestion which I would have had a lot of trouble refusing. Another! But the last.

We didn't talk much in the train, the old boy wanted to keep his trap shut. He kept his eyes fixed on the window for hours on end, until it got dark on the outskirts of Pisa. I tried to look for the leaning tower but he told me not to bother. I did everything I could to get him to take the plane. Bearing in mind his age, a one-hour journey seemed like a good idea to me. Not to him.

He wanted to stay in Sora for three days before we left, to be sure he wouldn't ever hear this whole business mentioned again in his life. When we left Mangini's house, Porteglia rang the emergency services, and we came across them as we drove away. The mass had just finished. Sant'Angelo had become an official saint, and his wine a holy nectar. The people from the Vatican were waiting for me round the corner. I agreed to their conditions, in every last detail, and from that moment on my father and I just did as they said. The Cadillacs suddenly disappeared off the face of the earth. No one saw them hanging around Sora any more. And I was almost worried about that.

Mangini disappeared – everyone was talking about it in the village the very next morning. No one knows how he explained the bullet in his ribs. An accident, perhaps. If he'd died everyone in the village would have come to terms with it. Old Cesare could have got the *compare* in the heart, I'm sure of it. You'd have thought he'd just wanted to shorten his life a bit. Or had he wanted to avoid finishing him off in front of me? When it came to it, did he find it too ridiculous shooting a man when he'd spent four long years avoiding doing just that?

Even I wouldn't be able to say exactly what sort of tacit agreement the two old boys had reached. I'll never know which of the two most wanted to see the other dead.

Still, my father can take pride in the fact that he does have some really good friends, at least two. One's a mate from his cure. They meet up every year, but this year he just sent my father some blank postcards of Perros-Guirec, which my father wrote and sent back to him so that he could then post them to us duly post-marked in the town. The other is Mimino, a childhood friend from Sora, who put him up and gave him all the information he needed without asking so much as a single question. He was just getting ready to confront Mangini when I pitched up in the village, and he put off the meeting until he'd found out what the hell I was up to there. He hardly set foot outside the whole time, and then only at night, in particular that night when Marcello made his revelations to me. I didn't need to ask him who'd knocked Porteglia out and then dragged me over to the chapel a bit later. Tough, my old man. You probably find hidden strength when you need to protect your brood. Hardly surprising such a tough old boot survived so much in the past.

I was sure he wouldn't answer the one really import-ant question. Because it led on to a thousand others, and I thought none of it was anything to do with me

185

either. I made up the answers for myself, and that was just going to have to do me. But I was free to imagine and embellish what really went on inside his head.

Now I understood why the old man didn't want to hear any mention of rigatoni for the rest of his days. The evening of Dario's funeral when I outlined the ingredients of that *all'albanese* recipe, he knew straight away who'd put it together. Ditto the land that Dario had just bought, my father knew all along who it had belonged to before. All he had to do was put the two pieces of information together to reach his conclusion. And he set off just like that, without letting us in on it.

Perhaps it was because Mangini was still alive forty-five years later and still capable of killing some kid, and knowing that had reignited a tiny glow buried under layers of ash. Perhaps he'd thought to himself that that kid could so easily have been me. Perhaps his motives were far more selfish than that. Perhaps what made him happy was settling his scores with the past. Perhaps he felt he no longer had anything to lose. And he felt he was making his last solo journey, his last little septuagenarian jaunt. Perhaps he was giving himself much more than that. A peaceful end. The ultimate relief. The final episode of that stupid, pointless war. Finally understanding why the man who'd been his companion through so much misery had chosen a different route at the last minute. Being reimbursed for an old debt before standing down.

Why didn't he get in touch with me when he knew I was in the village? Perhaps he thought that our two stories shouldn't overlap. Dario was my friend and Mangini was his. Or perhaps he knew that the two stories were going to converge anyway. Perhaps he felt that a son has to make his own revolution, that he's got his own things to defend, undertakings to honour and paths to tread. Or the memory of a friend who mustn't be betrayed.

And when it came to the crunch perhaps he thought that an old man like him did know, after all, when to take control, at what point to step in to stop a child burning himself when he's playing with matches.

Perhaps that's it.

I wanted to give him a meal in the restaurant car. He took out his sandwiches. We talked about money. He asked me what I was thinking of doing with my wad of lira.

"The money? . . . I don't know . . . if you've got an idea . . ." I managed.

"It's your loot, you earned it just the way you wanted to. Do you think it's clean?" he asked and then, a moment later, he added: "Do you want to be rich, then?"

"Pfff.. I dunno."

"I do."

After a long silence in which we abandoned ourselves to the rocking of the train I eventually asked him: "What is it you want?"

"New dentures, better ones, that really fit. To go on two cures every year. A dog. And . . . and that's all."

* * *

He went back to Vitry alone, as if he were coming home from Brittany, and I went home to Paris.

Paris, yes . . . I should have revelled in that moment. After so many different departures, at last a return. Catching my breath after my escapades. Coming back. One last time I drew on the one fairytale that had filled me with wonder through my childhood. As I carried on deeper into this country, it all came back up to the surface in spite of me. Because it had been there in me all along, buried deep down. Something halfway between a Greek tragedy and an Italian comedy. No one really knows which genre they're in any more: a drama in which you have to suppress the urge to laugh or a lighthearted farce which has a whiff of something more sinister about it. Neither a lament nor a lesson nor a moral. Just a disorientating tune, a hymn to the absurd, all-powerful in the face of common sense, a vision beyond happiness or sadness.

How I got home? . . . I met a couple of Albanians on the road, we were about eighteen miles from Tirana. They tended my leg as best they could. I limped and I've limped because of it for the whole of my life, but I walked on anyway. They gave me enough money to get to the harbour. And when I got there, you'll have to believe me, there was only one departure for Italy every month, and with my usual bad luck I'd just missed one by a couple of hours. I slept on the docks and joined some other poor devils in rags who'd managed to get that far like me. That went on for a whole month. I was dropped off in Naples, and there were so many Americans. I was ashamed to go home looking like a tramp, riddled with fleas and with hardly any clothes on my back. I met a Neapolitan who sold fake perfumes to the Americans: the stoppers smelled good but he filled the bottles with piss. I pretended to buy three, which was good publicity, and he took me on to keep playing the same trick. With the money I got cleaned up, bought some clothes and bought my ticket home. After four years. I was clean and smelled nice. I can tell you my fiancée was pleased . . .

I missed Bianca from the first moment I opened the door to my studio. And I can tell that's going to go on for a while. I'm going to miss that open coquettishness of hers. Her cheerfulness, her straggly slippers, her old-before-her-time housecoats, her red nail varnish, her stock of traditional stories and legends, her red lipstick, her soap opera dreams, her red cheeks, her gentleness, her tomato sauce and her outlandish humour. I'd like some local boy to find all those treasures one day, without taking them away. We promised each other that from now on we would celebrate our birthdays on the same day. A promise that won't be difficult to keep. That's the only way we found of growing old together.

To forget the fact that I'd come back I wanted to intoxicate myself with expensive pleasures, to give myself useless gifts, to drown myself in excessive luxury. I looked for ideas. An hour later I found myself at the end of the street, at the Restaurant Omar, enjoying an excellent couscous, anything rather than accept my surroundings.

The next day I went to visit my parents, and the old man and I play-acted a reunion very convincingly. My mother was completely inspired when I told her there had been a miracle in the village. When I took out a bottle of our own wine she crossed herself reverently and drank it till it made her head spin. My father didn't touch it. The others came: Giovanni, the eldest, then Clara, Anna and Yolande, my three sisters. I signed cheques for everyone, just to get rid of the money as soon as possible. Mamma Trengoni came by to see us. We talked about the vineyard and the miracle, but she didn't really understand. I took out some wads of notes for her rather awkwardly, but she was wary. I left it to my parents to explain it to her, to get her to accept the money and to encourage her to live somewhere a bit more decent. Sora, for example.

Just opposite, Osvaldo's house had grown like a mushroom. Urgently. Forcefully. Dying to get the roof over the ground. In just a month. All on his own. Standing proud and steady, he waved to me through the window.

In spite of everything, I could tell that my father was a bit quiet. He didn't want to get up from the table all afternoon, and normally he can't bear to stay inside for more than an hour at a time. My mother and Dario's mother were fascinated, hanging on my every word and asking for more and more details of the miracle and Marcello's healing. By the end they were almost thinking of making the pilgrimage.

I made the most of a moment alone with the old man to ask: "What's the matter?"

"It's my leg."

Hardly surprising. He missed out on his cure this year, and that's the only thing that helps him forget this last reminder of the war which he can't quite shake off.

"Does it hurt?"

He raised his arms to the heavens and said: "No, and it worries me."

Mother returned radiant. "This particular cure really did your old man a lot of good."

I seemed to be understanding less and less about what was going on. The old boy got to his feet.

And for the first time in my life I saw him walking without a limp, going up and down the room and shifting his weight from one leg to the other like Fred Astaire.

"A real miracle, that cure was," he said.

* * *

As I walked into the courtyard of my building I was having fun making plans for the money I had left. I thought about end-to-end holidays. As I put the land-ing light on, I was thinking about an endless holiday in a series of magnificent hotels. In the lift, I imagined all sorts of unrealistic scenarios. It was only when I turned the key in my door that I heard the quick muffled footsteps from the stairwell.

A stranger's face. I instinctively knew he was looking for me.

He came right up to me. As close as he physically could. Definitely too close.

Something clicked inside my head. The crossroads between the surprise that's already been and gone, and the fear that's now charging past. I thought I might be able to say something, to negotiate, show him my empty hands, and admit how tired I was, to trust in his good sense, and catch my breath a while before this whole thing got under way.

But his hand flicked too quickly in the pocket of his raincoat. Mine fidgeted with the key; the door refused to open.

I made a slow movement in his direction. As if to ask him to wait.

To wait to understand, before everything fell apart. Just for a fraction of a second, a scintilla, a little snatch of the truth. I felt like telling him we had all the time in the world. Time for him to tell me where he was from and who had sent him to me. Just out of curiosity.

Who is it that still wants me dead?

Right there, that was when I understood it would never be over. That it had all gone too far for it to end on my doorstep. That after such a feast of rancour and revenge and madness, there was still plenty left for another sitting.

He seemed surprised for a moment, then he slowly took out his gun which was equipped with a silencer.

191

Can't we put this off till later? Can't we have one last good time? Never mind. I wanted to warn him. Yes, to warn him, to tell him that – if I was fucked anyway – I was ready to ask for more.

He cocked his gun and I rolled to the ground. I launched myself at the stairs and a bullet whistled past my ear. I crawled up the steps, he followed me. A door opened somewhere in the distance and he turned to look.

And in that brief moment, that split second, my insides were suddenly gripped with hunger. Hunger.

To guzzle a whole slab of hatred, a longing for something red, for flesh. To devour every moving thing after so much fasting and impotence and regret. The regret of having been through too much, the menace and the death threats, the fear that I'd been given some lethal dose. I couldn't contain an extraordinary appetite for cruelty.

All that in the second that he hesitated.

I cried out once more as I threw myself at him. We rolled to the ground. The light went off automatically. He hit me with the butt of his gun on the top of my head but I didn't feel a thing – I'm going to eat him up here and now. I pushed him into the stairwell to stop him doing it again. He hurtled down the stairs and I threw myself on top of him. He fired the gun in the air right next to my mouth. I took his wrist in my mouth and bit as hard as I could, screwing my eyes up. He yelled with pain as he dropped the gun. But that wasn't enough for me.

Without loosening my grip with my teeth I picked up the gun and threw it well behind me. When I felt his blood stream over my tongue I opened my mouth. He got back up, clumsily, and ran down to the floor below in the dark. I couldn't bear for him to get away from me. I caught up with him by jumping down a floor. The feast wasn't over yet.

I stuffed him, sliced him, minced him up and larded him with blows until the juice oozed out of him.

"Let's eat!" I bellowed, my lips dripping with saliva.

He had the strength to scream and beg for mercy. A scream that would quell any appetite. I came back to my senses, almost satiated.

"For pity's sake! I beg you, for pity's sake . . ."

The word had an odd ring to it. When he saw me getting to my feet his whole body relaxed as if he were dead. His stomach heaved convulsively and I waited until he was ready to speak.

"Stop . . . I'm going to die . . . They didn't tell me . . ."

"Didn't tell you what?"

"That I had to take care of a madman . . . But you didn't look like one, just walking along the street . . . I wasn't on my guard, I thought with a gigolo everything was in the smile and the nice manners . . . How wrong I was . . . I end up with a bloody cannibal . . ."

I sat down on the stairs, too surprised to move. I didn't really understand what he'd just said. There was something I wasn't getting . . . I tried to search through my memory for all the factions of that voracious pack who each wanted their share of the cake.

"Parini?" I said.

"What?"

"Mangini?"

"Dunno him."

"What about Sora, d'you know Sora?"

"Who the hell is she?"

Something's not right here. This is all getting seriously confused.

"You've already tried to do me in once. From the club across the street."

"From a hundred feet away, that's about as close as anyone should get to you . . . Like a bloody idiot I missed you, so this evening I thought I'd try at point-blank range, and I end up nearly dying . . . Look, couldn't we go in, to your apartment? You haven't got a bit of disinfectant and the odd bandage, have you?"

"Are you being paid in lira or in dollars? Tell me, you piece of shit!"

"Hey . . . give me a break. I'm being paid in francs and the whole lot's going to go on hospital fees."

"Are you taking the piss?"

"For pity's sake! Ask me anything, I'll tell you everything, I'll admit it all, I'll even hand myself in to the police, now, straight away, but for God's sake don't get angry!"

"Who paid you?"

"I haven't a clue, you never know who it is you're working for . . . They got in touch with me to bump off a little wop who hangs out at a night club on the Rue George-V and who's seeing some woman up there. I followed her, she came and picked you up at the night-club and you went and spent some time in an apartment on the Rue Victor Hugo. You went home and that's when I spotted the terrace. Things were looking pretty good so I thought: why not straight away? On the spot . . ."

"And then?"

"Then you disappeared. And I waited for you to come back. Because the contract still holds. Well, I mean . . . it still *held* . . ."

The automatic light in the stairwell keeps going off. And out there on the landing there's nothing. Not a sound. No one having a quick look. I could have skinned the guy and left his carcass by the rubbish chute and no one would have done a thing.

I'd driven everything out of my mind. It was because of this silent creature that I left France. I thought I'd seen the last of him. I've got to get out of here. Run away again. I tuck the gun into my belt. Why did I help him write that letter?

"Have you got a car?"

"Uhh ... yes ... a blue 504 convertible, will that do?"

We go out. His car is parked two streets away.

"Look," he says, "with the contract, as far as I'm concerned, I'll give up and give them back their money. If the others want to end up dead ... Where are we going?"

"You're not going anywhere."

I held my hand out, palm up. He put his keys into it. Without asking where he might find the car later.

I set off down the Rue de Rivoli.

The Up is only just opening. They let me in, they recognize me, the manager smiles at me.

"Have you thought about it, *ragazzo*? Are you looking for work?"

"I'd like to see Madame Raphaëlle. Right now."

"*Calma. Calma, ragazzo.* Who do you think you are?"

I grab him by his tie and drag him over to the corner where I spent a pretty bad ten minutes, but things have changed since then. I take out my gun and jab the silencer against his throat. His minders start fluttering. He asks them not to move and grabs the telephone.

"Who are you calling?"

"Her."

"In her studio?"

"No, at her husband's house. We have *una* code."

She answers, he says just one word and hangs up.

"She's coming," he says. "But *attenzione, ragazzo . . .* she's gotta problems at the moment."

"She's going to have to deal with mine first."

"You could wait for her outside, no? It doesn't look good for the customers."

She came in fifteen minutes later. They found us a quiet corner, a table well away from the stage. The lady had clearly not had time to get herself ready. Very little make-up. No perfume. Just a few bits of jewellery. I didn't give her time to pretend to be surprised.

"Who tried to kill me?"

"What are you saying?"

I gave her the details. She didn't make any pretence of surprise. Her eyes betrayed a hint of distress and terrible weariness. She took agitated little drags on her cigarette and asked for a drink. The singer's crooning voice carried over to us and she tilted her head to listen.

"It won't happen again, I swear, Antoine."

I felt as if she were gradually slipping away from me. As if she were forgetting me in favour of the singer.

"I didn't know he still loved me that much, you see?"

"*Who*, for Christ's sake?"

She said nothing. It was almost as if she wasn't there. At the worst possible moment. In less than two minutes, she had spirited herself away. The situation was completely absurd but I did realize that I could never compete with that young wop's heartbreaking lament. Delivering his *Ti amo Ti amo Ti amo* so feverishly, with such ardour.

"My husband."

I gave an aggressive little bark of a laugh. More out of surprise than genuine contempt. But she was no longer listening to me. Every expression on her face,

196

every twitch of her hands, every blink, betrayed how much she missed Dario.

"He had me followed for months. When I met you I didn't know that, I swear to you."

They filled her glass up. From where we were sitting we couldn't see the singer, but she still tried to a hundred times.

"Years ago now he told me that if I ever cheated on him he would have my lover killed. He was frightened of losing me, you see . . ."

I sat there in stunned silence for a long time, still not understanding, not really grasping what she'd just said. Then I took her by the arm and shook her hard in order to get her attention.

"And what have I got to do with all this?"

"Nothing, really . . . My husband knew I was seeing someone and, at first, he didn't try to stop me. He wouldn't have been able to, anyway. When Dario died, I swore I would never cheat on him again. But he didn't stop having me followed. When you and I met, he immediately thought I'd broken my promise. Put yourself in his shoes . . . knowing that once again I was with a . . ."

"With a what? A wop? A Dario?"

"Why not . . .?"

Yes, why not, after all. I probably wouldn't have got so mixed up in anyone else's dreams. So why not his bed, too. When's the bastard going to let me go . . .

"It's ridiculous . . . I nearly died because of . . ."

"You're not in any danger now. I'll explain everything to him, admit everything. Right away. I'm so sorry, Antoine."

We heard clapping. She turned her head to try once again to catch sight of the singer, and I took the

197

opportunity to slip away. I'm sure she didn't notice a thing.

Back outside I felt calm again. I wondered whether it wouldn't be better to wait just one night before going back to my studio.

On the opposite pavement I could see the porter of the George V by the revolving door. It reminded me of the days when my brother was a chimney sweep, when he used to look after all the chimneys in that prestigious place. He told us all about it, the suites, the waiters, the stars, the luxury, the lot. Like a dream.

The time had come to check whether everything he'd said was true.

*　*　*

At breakfast the following morning I started talking to a man who was getting bored waiting for his wife to come down from their room. He felt like chatting and asked me to join him at his table. He noticed that I said no to coffee after one quick glance at his cup.

"I suppose you're originally from Italy, aren't you?"

"Yes."

"So you know how to cook noodles."

The non sequitur was so surprising it made me smile.

"Noodles, no. Just pasta."

"Pasta, then, if you prefer . . . Do you know how to cook it?"

"Some types, yes. But pasta's far more than just a bit of carbohydrate in search of a sauce."

"What do you mean?"

"It's a whole universe unto itself, in its raw form, and not even the greatest chef can imagine all the metamorphoses it can undergo. It's a strange combination

198

of blandness and sophistication. There's the whole geometry of infinite curves and straight lines, of shapes and gaps. And the taste derives from the shape. How else can you explain the fact that people look down on this mixture of flour and water when it's one shape and adore it when it's another. That's when you realize that the roundedness has a taste of its own, that the long and the short have a taste, and the smooth and the ridged. There's something passionate about it."

"Passionate?"

"Of course. It's because life itself is so varied and complicated that there are so many different kinds of pasta. Each shape is related to a concept. Each one has its own story to tell. Eating a plate of spaghetti is like seeing all the confusion of someone lost in a labyrinth, an inextricable confusion of different directions, a tangled web. It takes patience and a bit of dexterity to sort it out. Look at the way a plate of lasagne is put together. All you see is the uppermost layer, the nice crusty, cheesy bit they want you to see. But our man wants to see what's going on underneath, because he's sure all sorts of things are being hidden from him deep inside. Only to discover that there may be nothing more than on the surface. But first he's got to look. He'll get lost and go through long dark tunnels, not knowing whether he'll find anything at the end. There's nothing in the world more hollow, more empty and more mysterious than a piece of macaroni. Ravioli, on the other hand, now that's got something to hide – you never know exactly what. It's an enigma in a chest that's never opened, a box which will keep our chap guessing at what it's hiding. Do you know, they say that originally ravioli was meant for sailors. It was used to wrap up leftovers of meat and minced up bits of pretty much anything in a thin layer of pasta, in the hope that the sailors wouldn't find out what they were eating."

"Really? What about tortellini, what's that meant to be? A ring, a wedding ring?"

"Why not just a circle? Like a story that has no end. Turning full circle. Setting off . . . only to come back right where it started."

BITTER LEMON PRESS
LONDON

Bringing you the best literary crime and *romans noirs* from Europe, Africa and Latin America.

Thumbprint   *Friedrich Glauser*

A classic of European crime writing. Glauser, the Swiss Simenon, introduces Sergeant Studer, the hero of five novels.

January 2004   ISBN 1–904738–00–1   £8.99 pb

Holy Smoke   *Tonino Benacquista*

A story of wine, miracles, the mafia and the Vatican. Darkly comic writing by a best-selling author.

January 2004   ISBN 1–904738–01–X   £8.99 pb

The Russian Passenger   *Günter Ohnemus*

An offbeat crime story involving the Russian mafia but also a novel of desperate love and insight into the cruel history that binds Russia and Germany.

March 2004   ISBN 1–904738–02–8   £9.99 pb

Tequila Blue   *Rolo Diez*

A police detective with a wife, a mistress and a string of whores. This being Mexico, he resorts to arms dealing, extortion and money laundering to finance the pursuit of justice.

May 2004   ISBN 1–904738–04–4   £8.99 pb

Goat Song   *Chantal Pelletier*

A double murder at the Moulin Rouge. Dealers, crack addicts and girls dreaming of glory who end up in porn videos.

July 2004   ISBN 1–904738–03–6   £8.99 pb

The Snowman   *Jörg Fauser*

Found: two kilos of Peruvian flake, the best cocaine in the world. Money for nothing. A fast-paced crime novel set in Malta, Munich and Ostend.

September 2004   ISBN 1–904738–05–2   £8.99 pb

www.bitterlemonpress.com